FRIENDSHIP NEVER ENDS

Alexandra Sheppard

KO
KNIGHTS OF

For Michael, my bestie for life

CHAPTER ONE

SUNITA

When we found out that Holly Dalton in Year Ten was throwing an epic end-of-year house party with a '90s fancy dress theme, the girls and I knew we had to go all out. The only reason I even got an invite was because Holly has a mega-crush on my big bro Anand (gag). So, as lowly Year Nines, we had to really earn our spot at the party. And we'd do that by creating the greatest fancy dress costumes that Northstone Academy had ever seen.

We spent weeks planning our outfit. Gifty made mood boards of different themes, the group chat was flooded with ideas, and our little foursome nearly had our first ever argument when it came to deciding what we'd finally do. We didn't actually fall out, though. Like May's mum says, we're as 'thick as thieves.' I thought she was insulting our intelligence until May explained it means we are super close.

Then, inspiration struck in the bath. Just call me Archimedes, or whichever dead white dude it was who jumped out of the tub yelling "Eureka!".

"I've got the best costume idea for Holly's party!" I yelled into a voice note in our group chat.

It. Was. Perfect. I had thought of something creative, original, and iconically '90s. Even better, there were exactly four of them in the group! No one else in our boring school would think of anything so brilliant. It was totally unique.

Luckily, my friends agreed. Our outfit wouldn't come cheap and it would take some serious arts and crafts know-how to bring it to life, but it would be worth it when we saw the look on everyone's faces at the party. We spent the last month of Year Nine buying brightly coloured felt, tin foil and thread. Gifty must've spent hours on her mum's sewing machine but the time spent was worth it: when we saw ourselves in the mirror for the first time, Dawn laughed so hard that she busted a seam and Gifty had to re-stitch it.

The first inkling that we'd maybe, possibly, taken our fancy dress idea too far was when I showed Mum. I heard her come back from the office; her keys jangling as she placed them on the counter, and the kettle flicking on as she made her usual cup of peppermint tea to wind down from her day at the law firm.

"Boo!" I yelled, jumping into the kitchen doorway.

She screamed so loud that it made *me* scream. And for three full seconds we just stood there, screaming at each other.

"Sunita, are you trying to give me a heart attack?" Mum said, clutching her chest.

"It's my fancy dress outfit for tonight's party. You like? It's a '90s theme, we're going as–"

"Yes, I can see what you're dressed up as. I take it you and the girls are going as the set?" Mum asked.

"Abso-tutely! Don't forget we're having a sleepover at Gifty's tonight. It's our last night out before you drag me to France for the summer."

Mum rolled her eyes. "You know, most girls would be thrilled to be spending the summer in a genuine chateau."

Maybe if it was just us, I thought. There was no point

3

saying it out loud – we'd had that argument before.

This summer was a big one. It was our first time, since our friendship began, that all four of us weren't spending the summer holidays together. No pooling our money together for the bowling alley, no sneaking into 15-rated movies at the cinema, and no horror movie sleepovers.

I was going to some tiny French village for several weeks with Mum, Anand and Bryan the Bore. It's not the first time we've been on holiday with Mum's boyfriend, but it'll be the first time he's bringing his son and daughter. We've never met them before, because they're usually banished to some boarding school in the Surrey countryside.

I have no idea what we'll talk about. I don't know anything about skiing and caviar or whatever it is posh people like to spend their money on. If Holiday Anand is just like At Home Anand, then he'll spend the entire trip with his nose in some pretentious book pondering the meaning of life. And getting annoyed with me for breathing.

Dawn was going to performing arts summer school in London, Gifty was visiting her grandparents in Scotland, and May was staying right here in Kent.

That's why it was so important to have a brilliant night at Holly's party. It might be the last laugh we had for the entire summer.

We got changed at Gifty's house and walked to Holly's party. Gifty's dad offered to give us a lift, but our costumes couldn't fit into the car. Sure, we got a few funny looks as we walked down the street. One kid cried in his pram so hard that his dad had to walk on the other side of the road.

"Is it just me, or are we getting quite a few stares?" Gifty asked nervously.

"Mate, we're dressed as the most iconic foursome of the twentieth century," I said. "Of course we're getting stares!"

We turned a corner. The houses morphed from rows of neat terraces to mini mansions with sprawling driveways and sculptured hedges.

"Wow," May said. "So Holly is *rich* rich."

"I heard that she has a jacuzzi *and* a swimming pool," Dawn said.

We found Holly's house (it was the biggest one in the street, just like she'd described it in her invite) and crunched down the gravelled driveway.

"Ready, girls?" I asked.

Dawn nodded. Gifty looked like she was gonna throw up and May pursed her lips so tight they disappeared, but they both sort of look like that most of the time anyway.

We walked down the driveway arm-in-arm and I reached for the buzzer. Holly opened the front door.

"EH-OH!" We said in unison. Well, Dawn and I said it with our chests. Gifty and May stopped after the first "eh."

Silence. I swear you could hear our eyes blink. Eventually, after what seemed like an eternity, Holly said something.

"Jesus, who are you?" she frowned.

"I'm Tinky-Winky, this is Laa-Laa–" Dawn began.

"Yeah, I know who you're meant to be," Holly said. "But, like, who are you? Do I even know you?"

"It's me, Sunita!" Holly's face was still blank, so I added, "Anand's younger sister."

That seemed to jog her memory. She actually fluffed her hair and looked around for him. "Oh, is Anand coming tonight then?"

I flashbacked to when I'd told Anand about Holly's party a few weeks ago: he muttered something about parties being "an exercise in narcissism" and shut the bedroom door in my face. He'd gotten so moody since starting Year Eleven.

"Erm, sure. He'll be here later," I lied.

She reluctantly opened the front door wider, and we stepped in. "Who are you meant to be dressed as?" Dawn asked.

Holly spun around on her platform heels and looked at Dawn like she'd asked why she was wearing clothes. She gestured to her black mini dress. "Isn't it obvious? I'm Posh Spice, duh!"

She led us through her mansion of a house and we followed, being extra-careful not to accidentally knock anything over with our cushion-stuffed bellies.

"You know, the fancy dress idea was more of a suggestion," Holly said, as she led us to the kitchen.

Trays of party food lined the counter in silver platters. The massive French doors led to the garden, where a DJ played 90s R&B and bartenders were mixing drinks behind a stainless-steel bar. People danced on the lawn and posed for selfies under a giant neon sign with the words 'Party Like It's 1999'.

Not one of them was wearing fancy dress. They all looked super glam, like they were dressed for a night out in London.

"Help yourself to food. Martin behind the bar will make whatever drink you like," Holly said. "Oh, and Sonia, tell Anand to come find me when he arrives."

"It's Sunita," I said, but I shouldn't have bothered. Holly had already started talking to someone else.

"We are literally the only people in costume. I want to crawl into a ditch and die," May muttered.

"We're already dead and this is hell," Gifty said.

Dawn rolled her eyes. "Come on, girls! Think of the hilarious story this will make in a few years," she said.

I was so grateful for her optimism in that moment.

"Not all of us dream of being stand-up comics or stage stars, you know," May said. "I'd quite like to get through my GCSEs without further humiliation."

"Oh, cheer up, May. You're always complaining about only being known as the girl whose parents run *Golden Lotus* takeaway. Now you're known as the girl who dressed as Po!" I said. "These costumes are the result of weeks of creative ingenuity. Gifty, you could totally put these designs in your art school portfolio."

Gifty blushed. "They did turn out pretty well."

"Yeah! We can't back out now, or else I sacrificed Mum's scatter cushions for nothing," Dawn said, patting her belly.

8

Even though we tried to make the best of it, the party went downhill from there. Holly glowered at us every time we caught her eye, as it became more obvious that Anand was a no-show.

I can't lie, I was a little upset. No one else seemed to see the funny side of our costume. No one appreciated the hard work that went into hand-stitching the felt or making the antennae out of papier-mâché. We were the pariahs of the party.

There were some real lowlights: when the DJ played the *Teletubbies* theme tune as we walked into the garden, when Gifty overheated and nearly fainted inside her Dipsy costume, and when we realised that going to the loo was impossible in our costumes and we'd just have to hold it in.

But the worst bit was when a few boys from our year (the only other Year Nines there, and that's because they were our school's football champions) spotted us.

"Don't I recognise you from somewhere?" Scott said. He was looking at May.

The rest of the party fell quiet. Scott Mallory was the best-looking guy in our year and had never once acknowledged our existence. Why now?

May flushed bright red, matching her costume.

"We're in the same Geography class," she mumbled.

"Nah, that's not it. You work at *Golden Lotus*, right? I almost didn't recognise you without the hairnet. How quickly can you get me a sweet 'n' sour chicken?" He turned to yell at his friends. "Oi, it looks like the Chinese takeaway is doing deliveries. What do you want?"

His friends laughed like hyenas. May pursed her lips and looked down at the floor.

My blood boiled. "Shut up!" I spat. It wasn't my wittiest retort but I was too angry to think of anything smarter.

"What are you gonna do? Thump me with your handbag?" Scott sneered, before walking back to his cackling friends.

"Are you alright, May?" Dawn asked.

May sighed wearily. "I guess. It's nothing I haven't heard before."

"It's nearly ten o'clock," Gifty said. "You know Mum and Dad are strict about curfews."

We left the party, ignoring the sniggers as we walked sideways through the back gate.

"That's another great thing about this costume," Dawn said, as we walked to Gifty's house. "It's nice and warm. We don't even need a jacket!"

Gifty smiled weakly. "That's sweet of you to say, Dawn. But we all know the costumes were an utter disaster."

We got to Gifty's house, immediately raced to the loo (we were *bursting*), and settled our sleeping bags into the living room. As we scrolled through Instagram and Snapchat it became clear that we weren't quite as ignored as we thought. In fact, we were infamous.

We were in the background of every single video and photo. They were captioned with things like:

"Who brought the toddlers?"

"Top entertainment at @hollyc's 90s party!"

Most of them just had loads of cry-laughing emojis.

My stomach twinged as I scrolled through the videos and photos. I couldn't stop scrolling even though it made me feel terrible.

"No wonder Holly was fuming," I said. "We made her grown-up party look like a CBeebies special."

"Do you think everyone will have forgotten about it by September? I can't deal with being *Golden Lotus* girl AND *Teletubbies* girl," May sulked.

"If they haven't, I'll be changing schools," Gifty said. "I hear Silverhill Secondary has a decent Arts department."

"Guys, don't you think we're being a bit dramatic?" Dawn asked. "I'm sure there will be fifty scandalous stories coming out of that party by tomorrow morning. We'll be old news."

"I'm sorry, girls. I thought it would be a laugh to do something unique," I said.

Dawn patted me on the shoulder. "Hey, it was a sick idea! It's not your fault that everyone in our school is so dull."

"We're going to be in Year Ten soon," May said. "Don't you think it's time we . . . grew up a little? I'm not saying we morph into a wannabe influencer like Holly Carter, but wouldn't it make our lives a little easier if we just blended in?"

"But the whole reason we're friends in the first place is because we never blended in," I protested. "Don't you remember our Year One class with Miss Faversham?"

Our primary school was a sea of white faces. The first moment I spotted May, Gifty, and Dawn, I felt a crashing sense of relief. Even though we all come from completely different ethnic backgrounds (Indian, Jamaican, Chinese and Scottish-Ghanaian – we're basically the United Nations), we bonded over the fact that we felt so out of place. From then on, we were each other's home and we've been besties ever since.

Gifty sighed. "Maybe blending in is the wrong phrase," she said diplomatically. "But we could make an effort to be a little more grown-up."

"What, like Anand and Holly? No thanks," I crossed my arms.

Then I remembered the looks on everyone's faces at the party. How uncomfortable it made me feel. Did I really want to feel like that for the rest of the summer with Bryan and his snobby kids?

"I think it's a good idea," Dawn said. "It might be fun to try being grown-up for the summer, especially in London."

"I'm not sure how much I can reinvent myself whilst staying here," May pondered. "I desperately need to live vicariously through you guys. Do something BIG, won't you? Fall in love, get a dramatic new haircut . . . something!"

I sighed. "Well, it's not like me to refuse a challenge. I'll try to be a bit more mature over the summer and report back. But don't expect me to start watching films with subtitles or eating olives, or whatever it is grown-ups do."

"We can FaceTime every day, right?" May asked.

Gifty shook her head. "Not me. Granny and Grandad's village has rubbish Wi-Fi. Apparently it only works in the kitchen and that's *if* you stand on a stool."

"Yeah, it's the same with my chateau. The walls are too thick," I said.

"I can, but only in the evening. My summer school schedule is pretty tight," Dawn said.

May plunged her face into a pillow. Very dramatic for her. "This is awful. I'm gonna have to talk to Jenny the entire summer. Mum will make me babysit her every day!"

"I have an idea!" Gifty said and left the room. She emerged with a stack of white cards and dropped them on the carpet. "We'll write each other postcards! Mum bought them for me so I could stay in touch over the summer. They're blank so we can illustrate them with whatever we like."

We divided the postcards between us evenly.

"We'll write each other every few days," Gifty said. "Bonus points if they're illustrated."

Dawn threw a pillow playfully at Gifty. "Hey, no fair! You're literally Picasso. I can barely draw stick-men."

14

Being without my best friends throughout the summer feels scarier than I want to admit. They're literally the only people I know who get me. And for the next month, the only thing connecting us all is a stack of postcards.

CHAPTER TWO

DAWN

"Are you sure you have your train ticket, darlin'?" Mum asked for the gazillionth time.

And for the gazillionth time I resisted rolling my eyes. "They're on an app, Mum," I said, holding up my phone. "It's one of the wonders of the modern age."

I was getting ready for my trip and Mum was in full over-thinking mode. Even more than usual. She'd packed me three different types of sandwiches, a flask of tea, and a multipack of crisps for the one-hour train journey. She made me promise to text her at fifteen-minute intervals until Auntie Pat met me at the train station (after that I only had to text her every hour).

I was heading to London for performing arts

summer school. Luckily, my dad's sister has a flat that's only a bus ride away from the school, so I was staying there for the next month. Mum had been saving up for ages so she could afford to send me to Bright Stars Academy but paying for accommodation too would've been a stretch too far. She'd worked so hard to give me this opportunity.

"And did you pack your homework? Just because you're at stage school, doesn't mean you get to ignore your other subjects," Mum said.

"Yes, Mum. I simply can't wait to submerge myself in algebra and physics!" I said sarcastically.

Mum leaned in to give me a hug, like she'd been doing randomly over the last few weeks. "I'll even miss your cheekiness. This house is going to feel so strange without you here, sweetness," she said. "Dad would be so proud of you."

Performing runs in my blood. Mum and Dad met in a lovers' rock band (he was guitar, she was vocals) and it was their life. I was even named after Dawn Penn, their musical idol. When other kids went to see *Peppa Pig Live*, I was in the front row of reggae gigs in tiny South London cafes watching Dad play and Mum sing. They took turns on stage so one of them could hold me. It was our dream to sing on stage together when I was older. A dream Dad talked about for so long that I wasn't sure if it was his or mine.

Then, cancer happened. I was six so I don't remember much. It felt like one day he was here, jammin' on his guitar in the back garden and annoying our uptight neighbours. The next. he was gone. There was a whirl of friends and relatives in our tiny house, packing it out with delicious Jamaican food and fond memories. Then it was just me and Mum.

That's when she decided to leave the music gigs behind and train as an accountant. I think a part of her dreams died when we lost Dad. It's why she's so keen for me to pick up the family's musical legacy, to succeed where they failed.

"I was looking through your timetable for the next month," Mum said, cupping her mug of tea. "Street Dance, Pop Singing, Musical Theatre . . . You are going to have the best time! I already circled the classes I think you'll like the most. I think you should focus on the singing lessons, really master how to project your voice."

As Mum continued talking about how I needed

to work on my vocal range, my heart sank. I love performing. I love singing and acting and being on stage. Above all, I love making my family proud. So why am I dreading this summer?

Mum waved me off at the train station and that's when it hit me. I was on my way to London by myself! I found my seat on the packed train, unwrapped sandwich number one (tuna mayo and cucumber – a classic) and put on my Disney Musicals playlist. It was like my comfort blanket in audio form. The opening bars of The Lion King's *Circle of Life* blared through my phone, and that's when I realised my earphones weren't connected.

"Oh crap!" I hissed.

I dropped my sandwich and scrabbled to turn down the music, but it was too late. The entire carriage silently stared at the gangly fourteen-year-old girl playing Disney songs. The older girls on the table seat next to mine giggled to themselves, then went back to their phones.

Why is it that everyone but me thinks musicals are silly? Even Mum doesn't understand why I begged for *Hamilton* tickets for last Christmas. There's a Musical Theatre class at the academy but it clashes with the singing lessons Mum thinks will be good for me. Maybe next year.

*

Forty-five minutes. That's how long I waited on the train platform for Auntie Pat. I sat on my suitcase and scanned the crowd for any sign of her face. I rang her phone countless times.

Then, finally, she answered. Apparently, my cousin Kiana was meant to pick me up because Auntie Pat's shift at the hospital had run over.

"I'll text you the address and you can meet me at home, sweetheart. It's an easy tube journey from King's Cross," she said over the phone.

I gulped. I'd never taken the tube alone – or navigated using a map for that matter. Mum wouldn't like it, either.

"Sure thing, Auntie Pat," I croaked.

I hung up and began my adventure.

It turned out that navigating the tube with a giant suitcase in the summer heat was nearly enough to make me jump on the next train back home. If this is what being a grown-up is, then I don't want it. On the walk from Camden tube station to Auntie Pat's house, I silently cursed Kiana for leaving me stranded. When I finally found their flat, I was sweat-drenched and close to tears. I felt like I'd run an obstacle course with a wheelbarrow.

But my frustration melted away the second Auntie Pat opened the door. The woman standing in front of me was shorter than me (not difficult, I was the tallest girl in my year), and the ghost of my dad's smile danced on her face. It felt so familiar.

I was always closest to Mum's side of the family and so I spent Christmas and Easter with them. I hadn't seen Auntie Pat in years, not since Dad died. Yet somehow those years apart just drifted away.

"Look at my superstar niece, all grown!" Auntie Pat said before bundling me into a hug. She came up to my shoulders. "When did you get so tall, Miss?"

"About a year ago," I said.

"Lanky just like your father," Auntie Pat said. "And I hear that's not all you inherited from him. Where's your guitar?"

Ah. The infamous guitar. Even though I have a pretty decent voice, just like Mum and Dad, I didn't inherit the same passion for musical instruments. Mum tried and tried, going through every guitar tutor in a ten-mile radius. But I just didn't have the aptitude for it. Mum said she didn't mind, but I could tell that I disappointed her by being rubbish at it.

"Oh, I don't play that any more. I prefer the singing," I said.

Auntie Pat helped me to squeeze my suitcase through the narrow corridor. The smell of something delicious wafted from the kitchen and made my mouth water, despite my trio of train sandwiches.

"You'll be sleeping on the sofa bed, dearest, but you can put your clothes in Kiana's room. I asked her to make space in her wardrobe for you, but she has more outfits than Camden Market," Auntie Pat muttered. "I'm sorry she didn't meet you at the station as planned. That girl is a law unto herself."

I sat with Auntie Pat in the kitchen as she finished cooking dinner. She rolled and fried dumplings, her kind eyes flashing while she brought me up to date with the family gossip. Then we heard the front door slam, followed by another door slamming. A few seconds later, loud drill music vibrated through the walls.

Auntie Pat rolled her eyes and wiped her hands on a tea towel. "Excuse me, darlin'."

The music turned off and Auntie Pat came back to

the kitchen, trailed by an older girl: my cousin Kiana. I vaguely remembered meeting her at dad's Nine-Nights before his funeral. But the mature sixteen-year-old with a waist-length weave and perfectly man-icured nails was nothing like the little girl I'd met all those years ago. My fave comfy pink tracksuit and simple afro puff suddenly felt babyish in comparison.

"I think you owe your cousin an apology," Auntie Pat said.

"Mum, I already told you that I was working at the shoe shop today," Kiana said. "I asked for extra shifts over the summer, remember?"

Auntie Pat said nothing, only fixing her with The Stare that all Caribbean mums seem to have inherited.

Kiana sighed and finally looked at me. "Listen, I'm sorry yeah, but we live like two stops from the train station. I thought you were old enough to manage that alone."

"I am," I said. For some reason my voice came out all squeaky and high.

Later that evening, we ate dinner on the small kitchen table. Kiana and I were silent, but Auntie Pat chatted enough for the both of us. Which was fine with me, as I wanted to focus on the food; I had seconds and thirds of the delicious curry chicken.

"I bet you haven't heard this in years!" Auntie Pat said and came back with a small CD in her hands. "It's one of your dad's early demos. I found it when I was doing a clear-out."

"Oh mum, no one wants to hear that dead music," Kiana said.

Dead.

Kiana's brown skin turned red at the cheeks. "Sorry . . . I didn't mean it like that."

"I'm sure Dawn would love to hear this," Auntie Pat said. She slipped the CD into an ancient-looking stereo on the kitchen counter and pressed play.

It was definitely an early demo. The recording quality was poor, and the melody sounded like it was played on a toy keyboard. But my dad's voice sang soulful and true; my earliest audio memory.

I didn't miss him most of the time. I know that sounds harsh, but I was so used to it being just Mum and me. But in that moment, the love I had for him flooded like a burst dam. I had to hold the tears back. Suddenly I understood why Mum wanted me to keep his legacy alive – so she could hold on to a piece of Dad forever.

Surely honouring that dream was the least I could do?

"You don't actually like that ancient music, do you?" Kiana asked me.

Weird. No one had ever asked me that before. It was always assumed I did. That I'd follow in Mum and Dad's footsteps.

"Of course she does!" Auntie Pat said. "The girl is a star in the making."

Kiana shrugged. "I didn't think people our age were into that."

It warmed me that she described us in the same age bracket. I sat up a little straighter. "Actually, I really like–"

My phone rang. It was Mum. I hadn't text her in about three hours.

"Sorry, I should take this," I said. But Kiana had already stopped listening.

*

It was my first day at Bright Stars Academy. Luckily, I didn't have to agonise over my outfit: the uniform was black trousers and a black t-shirt emblazoned with the school's logo. As I showered and dressed,

I thought of all the grown-up things I'd already done in the last twenty-four hours. I'd never taken the train or tube by myself before. I got the feeling that Auntie Pat was considerably more chill than Mum. The weird thing was, I wasn't sure if I liked that. I had gotten so used to Mum's over-protectiveness that being without it felt like sleeping without a duvet.

Auntie Pat helped me find the school on Google Maps the night before, so all I had to do was follow the directions to the bus stop and go from there. It sounded easy but the nerves had my stomach in knots. I couldn't eat the cornmeal porridge Auntie Pat left for me on the stove.

I suddenly realised that I was about to start singing, acting, and dancing in front of complete strangers.. It was one thing doing it in Mr Arnett's Drama class at school, where I had known everyone for years (and, let's face it, was the best singer by far), but now I was going to a place where people had trained. Some of them went to stage school every day, not just during the holidays. I was no longer the big fish in the little pond that was Northstone Academy.

I left the empty flat (Auntie Pat was at work and

Kiana was . . . who knows) and wandered through the streets of Camden towards the bus stop. Even though it was early, the sun was high in the sky and the market traders were setting up for the day. In my bad mood yesterday, I hadn't noticed how much there was to take in. I spotted half a dozen different food stalls I needed to try and interesting shops I wanted to browse. It was May's birthday later that month and I decided right then that her birthday present would be something uniquely London from this market.

A notebook stall caught my eye and I stopped to browse. No one I knew loved stationery more than May. Maybe I could get her a new notebook for her collection?

My phone buzzed. It was a good luck text from Mum, but I didn't reply because I caught the time.

Registration started in ten minutes. *Yikes!*

I dropped the notebook and ran towards the bus stop, my rucksack slapping against my back. This was not the cool and collected start to my Bright Stars career that I'd envisioned for myself.

I arrived at the Academy a hot mess. The school was located down some weird side-street in a neighbour-hood called Soho. It was impossible to find. I tried asking for directions, but people either shrugged at me or gave me overly complicated instructions. When I saw the street sign and ran down the alleyway, I nearly cried with relief when I saw the school's sign above the door.

I checked the time. I was more than an hour late. How on earth did that happen?! Did time run differently in London or something?

The receptionist directed me to the room for my singing lesson. I walked down the winding corridors, the sound of singing and tuning instruments jostling with one another. Just as I found the room for my singing lessons, something else caught my ear. I turned around and moved towards the source of the sound, down a dark corridor.

The sound grew louder. I recognised it immediately: it was the opening bars of my favourite song from my favourite musical. Mum took me to see *The Lion King* for Christmas a few years ago and, no word of a lie, it was the best day of my life. When I tried to sleep that night it was impossible. I kept on replaying my favourite scenes from the show in my head.

At the end of the corridor was a door, that opened to a small auditorium. About two dozen teens were on the stage dressed in black and they were singing the song I loved so much. I walked down the aisle as if in a trance. The song finished and I had to stop myself from clapping.

A man standing below the stage, dressed in a Bright Stars Academy t-shirt, looked up from his notes. "Needs work," he said bluntly.

I gawped at him. It was the most sublime thing I'd ever heard, and it was from people my age. How could he not have been impressed?!

The man must have sensed my stare because he turned to look at me. "You're late," he said in the same nonchalant tone.

"Sorry!" I blurted out. "I'm not meant to be–"

"What, forty minutes late to my class? I should think not. But I'll overlook it on the first day. Join the others, please."

My heart jumped to my throat. Was I really joining a Musical Theatre class? Was I really skipping the singing lessons that Mum so badly wanted me to take? Before I had a chance to think about the implications of what I was doing, I dumped my rucksack on the floor and stepped onto the stage.

Dear May,

The academy is not what I expected. I thought it would be like school but with more singing, but it's way cooler. My teacher is a bit of a dragon, though. The drawing on the front of this postcard is a perfect recreation of the moment I walked into his class forty mins late. No, the googly eyes are not an exaggeration.

I hope life at home isn't too dull. Knowing you, you've found a way to pass your time that is both interesting and efficient. I know you won't stay bored for long.

Say hi to Jenny for me!

Big hugs, D x

P.S. I've already bought your birthday present, so expect a parcel from me in a few weeks.

CHAPTER THREE

MAY

I am beyond pathetic. I spent the first few days of the summer holidays checking the post for any news from my friends. Dawn checked in on me a few times via text, but our group chat just isn't the same without Gifty and Sunita too.

It's just my luck that my friends all decided to have exciting summer trips at exactly the same time. Me? I'll be lucky if I leave Kent. At least I'll earn some extra cash working in the takeaway, so the summer won't be a complete waste of time.

I even tried a more grown-up hairstyle. I usually wore my long black hair in two plaits: it made life easier at the takeaway, and I'd done it for so long it was on autopilot. But I decided to try something new.

I stood in front of the bedroom mirror and scraped it into a sleek high ponytail, like Ariana Grande. I kind of liked it, but Jenny laughed when she saw it.

"Good luck getting that into a hairnet," she said.

I gave her the evil eye. "Just wait until you have to work at the takeaway."

My grown-up reinvention didn't stop at the hair-style. I wrote in my journal about all the ways I could make myself more mature, like drinking warm lemon water to improve my skin and remembering to water the plants on my windowsill. I read this self-help book Dad likes and it said that little changes are the best way to improve. I started with a sip of lemon water and nearly wretched, but that's okay. Tomorrow morning, I'll take two sips.

When Dawn's postcard arrived, I pounced on it like a hawk and read it greedily. Her London life sounded so glamorous! I would be terrible at stage school. I can't put my hand up in class without blushing. Not for the first time, I wondered what it must feel like to go through life with the confidence of Dawn and Sunita.

I kept the postcard in my pocket so I could have it close to me at all times, and also so Jenny wouldn't find it. My eleven-year-old sister was in this weird snooping phase. Now that our big brother Andy was back home from university for the summer, I'd had to move out of his room and back into the bunkbed I shared with Jenny. Neither of us was happy about it.

Spending my entire summer with her was going to be a challenge. I'd rather work double shifts in the takeaway than babysit Jenny, but Mum said child labour laws won't allow it. I can work a maximum of twenty-five hours per week. I don't actually mind working at the takeaway, especially when all my friends are on adventures. I'd just be sitting at home anyway.

Still, looking after Jenny was better than the time my weird cousin Tim from Ohio came to spend the summer with us when I was twelve. He insisted that outer space was "fake news". He also refused to eat any of Mum's home-cooked food and lived on toast for the entire summer.

My friends told me I should consider myself lucky to have a summer job – they all have to rely on pocket money from their parents in order to do anything fun. But ever since Scott Mallory and his annoying friends recognised me at the party, I felt self-conscious. Well, even more than usual. The last thing

I wanted was someone from school to come in when I was behind the till.

But, because this is my life we're talking about, that was exactly what happened.

It was a typical slow Thursday afternoon, and I was sneakily reading a book while standing at the till. When it's slow there are other jobs I could do (watering the jade plants, bagging up prawn crackers, wiping down the counter), but I was in the middle of this mystery novel I'd discovered on TikTok, and the plot was getting juicy. I was so engrossed that I didn't hear it before it was too late: the familiar honking laughter of teen boys as they approached the takeaway.

I looked up, but I knew who it was before I saw them. Of course it was Scott Mallory and his friends. Of. Course.

I did the only thing that made sense to me at the time: I ducked. I crouched under the counter, curled into a ball and hid like a ten-year-old playing hide and seek. Truly, my ingenuity knows no bounds.

"Helloooo? Anyone here?" One of the boys said.

A few seconds passed. I heard the kitchen door swing open and Mum emerged. "May, where are you? We have customers waiting!"

She sighed dramatically when she saw I was nowhere to be found and reluctantly talked to the boys. "I'm sorry, my daughter is meant to be serving customers. What can I get you?"

Please don't see me. Please don't see me.

The only thing more embarrassing than Scott and his bonehead mates teasing me for working here would be them finding out I was hiding from them. Mum took their orders and it felt like hours. I stared intensely at her Crocs, praying that she wouldn't accidentally tap me with her toes.

"Food ready in fifteen minutes, okay?" Mum said.

"Cool, we'll wait," one of them said.

That fifteen minutes felt like a year. My bum ached from sitting against the hard floor and my neck ached because it was turned at a funny angle. For the second time that week, I mused about how I'd walked myself straight into the path of humiliation. Why didn't I just hide in the loo or something?

I heard them mention Holly's party and I strained my ears to hear what the boys were talking about, but they didn't bring up the fancy dress costume or the silly girl wearing it. In a way, that hurt even more. I wasn't memorable even after the most embarrassing moment of my life.

I didn't need to hide under the counter. I was invisible anyway.

After what seemed like an eternity, Mum emerged from the kitchen with carrier bags of food. "Thanks boys, see you soon," she said.

The boys left with barely a word of thanks (rude), and I allowed myself to relax. I made it! Unlike Holly's party, this was one incident that would stay between me and my journal.

"Get up now, May," Mum said as she walked back into the kitchen.

Crap.

*

It was a Sunday night and the takeaway closed early so Mum and Dad could welcome Andy home. They celebrated by making his favourite steamed sea bass, then berated him for every life choice he'd made since graduating high school. Our parents seem to think that his problems stem from the fact he was doing a History degree instead of training to be a lawyer, doctor or accountant. Heck, they'd even have been happy with an optician.

I know it makes me sound like a disloyal sister, but I was secretly relieved. If Andy was getting a hard time, it meant that Mum wouldn't bring up my disappearing act at the takeaway a few days earlier.

"How's school going, May? Looking forward to your GCSEs?" Andy asked, looking at me hopefully. He was desperate for a change in the subject.

I shrugged. "Yeah. I guess."

Dad smiled broadly. "May had an excellent report this year. She's our future mathematician."

I smiled weakly. Dad has it in his head that I'll be studying Maths, or something equally as practical, at university. He's started his campaign from the moment Andy decided to change his degree from Economics to History at the eleventh hour. Dad was so disappointed. Why would his eldest son want to spend time in the past when he could be looking to the future?

The thing is, I haven't worked up the guts to tell Dad that I won't be studying Maths at A-Level, let alone doing an entire degree in it. I can get my head around algebra and geometry, but it's an unsatisfying slog. What I really want to do is a Creative Writing course, but that would be out of the question.

Though the living room bookshelf is stacked with

books about business and commercial law, the idea of reading for fun is alien to my parents. So is the idea of doing anything for fun, for that matter. Their idea of leisure time is doing their business tax returns in front of an old episode of *Countdown*.

"Jenny, no phones at the table!" Dad said sternly.

"Sorry. It's just that someone at May's school went viral!" she said.

"No way. Who?" I demanded.

Jenny put her phone back into her pocket. "Some girl in Year Seven decided to start her own lemonade stall. It was so popular, she ended up bottling it and selling it all over the country!"

That got Mum and Dad's attention. "Hmm, clever girl," Dad said approvingly, before returning to his noodles.

"Much better than spending the summer holidays wasting time on her phone," Mum added.

After dinner, I took a break from loading the dishwasher to find this girl Jenny mentioned. I scrolled through her videos and read the comments beneath them – people were really going nuts for her lemonade! One video saw her boxing up hundreds of bottles to ship around the country. She must be raking it in.

I couldn't help but feel a little disappointed. My short-lived BookTok account where I reviewed my favourite reads only got a handful of views (mostly thanks to my friends), and Lemonade Girl went viral on her third video. Where was I going wrong?

*

During my lunch break at the takeaway (I always arrived at the takeaway early so I could join the family meal, where Mum and Dad made food for the staff – today it was a delicious clay pot rice), I took out my journal and began brainstorming ideas.

If Lemonade Girl could make money in the summer holidays, then why couldn't I? But, if I was being honest with myself, it wasn't just the money that appealed. It was the reinvention of my image as nerdy May. Besides, isn't this what the girls and I talked about just last week? I was sick of going through school not being noticed. Or being noticed for all the wrong reasons. If I could reinvent myself as an entrepreneur, then maybe I would be seen for once. And, if the business really took off, Dad would get off my back about that Maths degree. I was going to study English or, if I worked up the courage in time, Creative Writing.

I drummed my pen on the small plastic table in the takeaway. Lucas was on shift now and I didn't start for a few hours, so I had plenty of time. Lucas was the first and only person outside of our family that my parents hired, and he was also from one of the few families in this town who weren't white. But people didn't seem to care that he was Nigerian because he was so good at football. At least, that's how it looked to me.

He was a year older than me, but not like the other older boys I came across; he was actually nice. I guess it pays to be friendly to the daughter of your employers.

I don't know why he chose to work at the takeaway. Most teens get summer jobs at the retail park or in a cafe, not somewhere where they end up smelling permanently of oil. Still, here he can have all the prawn toast he could possibly want. You don't get that at JD Sports.

"Finally writing that novel, May?" he asked.

I'd let slip about my writing ambitions on one slow shift, when Lucas stayed late to keep me company. I rolled my eyes, but I was secretly pleased he remembered. "I wish I'd never told you about that."

"Well, I'll keep bringing it up until you actually start it," he said.

"If you must know, I'm trying to come up with a business idea," I said. "A girl in my school went viral for making lemonade!"

Lucas raised his eyebrows. "Must be some special lemonade! What ideas do you have so far?"

I shrugged. "Nothing. There's not much I am good at."

Gifty was the artistic one, Sunita was the funny one and Dawn was the talented one. I got good grades at school, but what kind of marketable skill was that?

"That's not true at all, May," Lucas said. "You helped me with my History coursework last term, remember? Anyway, what's wrong with working here?"

"Nothing!" I said, hoping my parents didn't hear. I wouldn't want to hurt their feelings by implying that I was too good for their business. "It's just not the most exciting thing in the world, is it? No one's going to go viral for working in a takeaway."

Lucas smiled, revealing his dimples. "Since when do you care about going viral?"

I blushed. It sounded so silly when he said it out loud.

41

Luckily I was saved by the bell: a delivery driver came in to collect a large order and Lucas jumped into action. I returned to my notebook and began a list of all the things I was good at:

1. Homework
2. Being on time
3. Following the rules

Wow. I sounded like a right laugh. It was a wonder I had any friends at all. Though I had a feeling that, if my friends were here, they'd have a tonne of nice things to say about me. They always knew the right things to say that made me feel better.

What would they say if they were here? One time, I made a really nice batch of brownies for Sunita's birthday. In fact, they were so good she ate half the tray in one go and had sugar deliriums for the rest of her birthday party.

The more I thought about this idea, the more it made sense. With Mum and Dad at the takeaway and Jenny at play centre, I had the house to myself outside of my shifts, not to mention a professional kitchen full of equipment. I could bake to my heart's content! And who doesn't love brownies?

I added a fourth point to my list:

4. Baking brownies

For the first time since my friends had left, I felt excited about what lay ahead for the summer holidays.

Dear Gifty,

I think this summer might be more fun than I'd ever hoped. I've decided exactly how I'm going to reinvent myself; when you get back from Scotland, expect to see a whole new May!

To say I miss you would be an understatement of the century. Every morning I wake up and it takes me a few seconds to remember that our foursome has been scattered to the winds.

I hope Scotland is everything you hoped for and more. How are the grandparents? I bet they can't believe how lucky they are to have such a talented, thoughtful grandchild. I bet you've wowed them with your creative flair without even trying.

I can't wait to receive your postcard! I expect it to be illustrated with something mind-blowingly original. I haven't even attempted to draw anything, as you've noticed, but I am sending you hugs from across the border.

Yours forever, M x

CHAPTER FOUR

GIFTY

In primary school we'd learned about kids sent to stay with people in the countryside during World War Two. They were called evacuees. That's a little how I felt when I stepped off the train at Glasgow Central Station. Even though Mum and Dad weren't off fighting a war, I felt a stab of empathy with those kids leaving the train to start a new life with strangers.

Granny and Grandad technically weren't strangers, but they may as well have been. Apparently, I met them when I was a baby and there was a photo on our mantelpiece to prove it: me, a new-born with a shocking mop of black curls, being held tightly by a grinning middle-aged white woman while

Grandad stands besides us both, unsmiling.

I'm not used to being around extended family. I'm not used to being around much family full stop, because of how far spread out everyone is. Mum's Scottish and Dad is Ghanaian, and that's where their families live. We always have Christmas Day just the three of us and I wouldn't want it any other way.

I was Mum and Dad's miracle baby. They tried for years and years and nearly gave up hope, but then I suddenly appeared just before Mum's forty-third birthday. They are the oldest parents at school, but I wouldn't trade them for anything. They're over-protective and always fussing. (Don't tell my friends but I secretly like it.)

It was why the trip this summer came as such a surprise. Mum doesn't like it when I take the bus to school alone, let alone a seven-hour train. But for some reason, Mum decided that it was time for me to connect with my roots and finally spend time with her parents in Scotland. They lived in a small town outside of Glasgow.

I knew basically nothing about them. The only contact I'd had with them was awkward phone calls on birthdays, where Granny asked how tall I was getting and whether I liked the tins of shortbread she sent in the post. Grandad was never around for these calls, but Granny could talk enough for both of them.

They met me at the train station. With Granny waving and loudly yelling from behind the ticket barrier, they were pretty hard to miss. They made a funny-looking pair. Granny was short and round with very pink cheeks that popped out when she smiled, which was often. Grandad was long and thin and didn't make a single sound apart from the rustling of his long trench coat.

Grandma bundled me into a tight rose-scented hug. Grandad shook my hand.

"You'll catch your death in that get-up!" Granny said.

I looked down at my denim shorts and t-shirt. "It was hot when I left home."

Granny chuckled. "Well, you won't have need for summer clothes here. I hoped you packed an anorak!"

Mum warned me about the rain in Scotland, but I thought she was exaggerating – like when she said being on my phone too much would give me radiation poisoning.

"I'm less concerned about the rain and more concerned about Gifty standing out," Dad said when

Mum brought it up. "Some of the villagers weren't too keen about me if I recall correctly. Remember the stares when we stopped at the pub?"

Mum rolled her eyes affectionately. "Oh, Isaac, that was twenty years ago. Times have changed!"

Dad and I exchanged glances. We both loved Mum, but she could be annoyingly clueless about how the world worked sometimes. Still, Dad agreed to let me go but said I was to book the first train home at the slightest hint of racism.

It wasn't the most relaxing way to start a holiday.

On the short drive home, Granny talked non-stop. It was actually kind of relaxing to have the background noise. I was grateful for it, especially since Grandad didn't say a word. I don't think he'd even looked at me since I arrived. Maybe wearing my hair curly was a bit much? My hair was a riotous mass of black curls. It made a statement whether I liked it or not.

We arrived at their cottage and Granny showed me to the spare room: Mum's childhood bedroom. I had to admit, it was adorable. It was small but perfectly formed. The paisley duvet matched the jug of lavender on the wooden bedside table. The window overlooked the rambling back garden, where there was an apple tree and a large shed. If my friends were here, we'd climb the apple tree and see who could get the highest without getting scared (my money would be on fearless Dawn).

But they weren't here. It was just me. I didn't get lonely very often, but now I released that was because I took my friends and family for granted. I'd never spent any time apart from Mum and Dad before. Even though I spent a lot of time in my room alone painting or sketching, I knew that Mum and Dad were just one room away. I could hear Mum singing along badly to Magic FM or Dad humming to himself as he shaved in the bathroom.

Here the house was silent, apart from the distant mooing of cows in the background. I unlocked my phone to see if there was any connection at all, but there were zero bars for data or phone reception. I couldn't even send Mum or Dad a text.

I opened the windows to let in the fresh country air and immediately regretted it. The country air smelt like manure and old cabbages, and it was freezing. Did Scotland forget it was meant to be July?

I decided to fill the time by unpacking my suitcase, which I did slowly and deliberately. My clothes were separated into two categories: my art clothes, stained with paint, chalk, and PVA glue, and my good clothes. My art clothes I folded into the rickety wooden chest of drawers while I hung my few good outfits on the clothes rail. I didn't have much of them, but that wouldn't be a problem here. It's not like I was going to dress up for the cows.

By the time I neatly arranged my clothes and folded them using the space-saving method May taught me (the girl was an organisation enthusiast), I was positive I'd killed the entire afternoon. I checked the time on my phone: it had used precisely forty-eight minutes.

This was going to be a long summer.

*

Granny called me down to dinner and asked me to set the table. The small kitchen table was clearly meant to seat two people comfortably, but they tacked on an extra chair and placemat for me. Grandad sat at the table and silently poured me a glass of water from the ceramic jug on the table. I'd been here for several hours, and he still hadn't said a single word to me. Mum had never mentioned he was this quiet. What was going on?

Granny handed me my plate which had salmon, a pile of green peas, roast potatoes, and a giant blob of a sticky-looking white mush.

"I asked Gillian what your favourite food was, and she said you were fond of rice," Granny said. "I've never cooked it before but luckily I had an old Delia Smith recipe."

"Thanks, Granny," I said. "Looks delish!"

I had to be polite. Granny looked so proud of herself. And Mum was right: rice is one of my favourite foods . . . when it looks like food and not papier-mâché glue.

Granny chatted, while Grandad ate silently and I pushed the massacred rice around my plate. If Grandad's quietness was unusual then Granny never let on. She talked and talked, and took it as quite natural that no one else was able to get a word in. It suited me just fine. Grandad's silence made me feel awkward and shy. Even more than usual.

While Granny chatted, I daydreamed about what my friends were up to. I imagined Dawn wowing the performing arts summer school with her incredible singing. Sunita was probably eating croissants and having her Mum's boyfriend's family in fits of laughter, while May was lucky enough to wake up in her own bed with her family in the next room. It had barely been one day, and I already missed my parents fiercely.

But then Granny announced it was time for dessert and suddenly I felt less lonely (sugar can have that effect on me). We had fresh raspberries from the garden with vanilla ice cream. Granny laid the bowls out in front of us, and I reached for the tub of ice cream. When Grandad thought I wasn't looking, he took a small handful of raspberries from his bowl and tipped them into mine. Maybe he didn't hate me after all.

After dessert I volunteered to do the washing up. Granny looked very pleased and said yes, sitting at the kitchen table while she watched me wash up. She decided that the plants in the window box needed watering and pottered around to do that. Even though she was in her eighties, Granny seemed like the sort of person who couldn't keep still.

"I've got a special treat for you, Gifty," Granny said, holding up a carrier bag.

I dried my hands on a chequered tea towel and delved into the bag. It was crammed full of arts and crafts materials: glue sticks, coloured card, poster paints, glitter glue, and even modelling clay. It must've cost a small fortune!

"Do you like it, hen? I remember all the drawings you used to send us every Christmas," Granny said.

I nodded. "It's perfect."

But, as I hauled my small sack of goodies up to my room, I couldn't help but remember what happened the last time I got carried away with an arts and crafts project. The party was just last week and the humiliation of it all still stung. Did getting excited about glue sticks and modelling clay make me a big baby?

I put the bag of arts and crafts materials under my bed. Just looking at it reminded me of the party, and I wasn't ready to relive that humiliation any time soon.

The next day Granny sent me to the village square to buy fresh bread for lunch and to get myself 'a little treat' with the change. There was exactly forty-seven pence left over, but Dad had given me a wad of emergency cash just before I left the house so I had spending money.

Sadly, there was nothing much to spend it on. The local corner-shop-slash-post-office had the saddest selection of penny sweets I'd ever seen. I walked back to the cottage with the unspent cash burning a hole in my pocket. I decided to take a different route home to mix it up a bit, and suddenly my phone began to vibrate in my pocket. I took it out and saw notifications begin to crowd the screen.

I had an internet connection! I nearly jumped for joy, but I managed to contain my excitement. I looked around to gauge my surroundings and realised this sweet spot between the antique shop and the old man pub was where I could get decent reception.

Sadly, my excitement was short-lived. Once I scrolled through the dozens of notifications from various apps, only a couple of them were from my friends. I guess they were too busy enjoying their summers to update the group chat. Would it look deeply pathetic if I broke the silence? I began to type out a message but stopped myself. What would I tell them anyway? Literally the most exciting thing I'd seen since arriving were the cows in the field outside my window. And there were plenty of those in Kent.

Even Mum and Dad didn't seem that interested. They'd only texted me once since I arrived. For all they knew, I could have been the victim of a major railway accident! I wished they'd adopted this relaxed attitude during our Year Eight school trip to Berlin.

Mum rang the teacher leading the trip so often that Miss Fruhstucke pretended that she'd left her phone at the hotel.

When it was clear that my phone wasn't about to erupt with messages and phone calls, I decided to trudge back to the cottage. I walked past the village square and noticed something I hadn't seen since arriving yesterday: people my own age. A small gang of girls lounged on the bench like it was a sofa in their house. They were chatting and laughing and messing about on their phones. It made me feel so much lonelier. I would've given anything to be back home lolling about with my friends on a random bench.

I must have been staring because one of the girls looked over, and the other two followed. I suddenly realised how different I looked to anyone else here. It was silly of me to assume that I could blend into the background and gawp at strangers. Not me with my brown skin and thick black hair.

The girl who sat in the middle, the one with light brown hair in a topknot, waved me over. They were all dressed in cropped t-shirts and jeans while I had my anorak wrapped closely around me. I couldn't get over the fact that this was meant to be summer and no one else here was cold.

I approached them, conscious of the fact that I was holding a loaf of bread like it was a small child. I tucked it under one arm in an attempt to look more casual. I could feel my cheeks beginning to burn, like they did whenever anyone talked to me at school and I wasn't expecting it.

Why can't you act normally for once, Gifty? Why are you constantly embarrassed? Why–

"Are you new here?" the girl with the topknot asked. "Don't think I've seen you before."

"Yeah, I'm new. I'm–"

The girls gasped. "She's English! Are you from London?" One of them asked.

"No way! Have you met celebrities? Do you shop at Oxford Circus?" Another one squealed.

I relaxed. This was actually the perfect encounter because I didn't have to say a thing. The three girls launched a volley of questions and comments at me so quickly that I didn't have time to answer. I did manage to say that I was in the village for the next three weeks visiting my grandparents. They couldn't believe I'd left London to stay there. I tried to tell them that I'm not actually from London, but they didn't believe me.

They introduced themselves as Isla, Megan and Skye.

"What's your name?" Isla asked. She was the one who'd called me over and I suspected she was the leader of their group.

"Gifty," I said.

They practically swooned. "It's so exotic," cooed Skye.

I smiled. "I thought the same about your name," I said.

Skye looked confused. "Nah, it's normal. Yours is anything but."

"Anyway, I'd better get home for lunch," I mumbled.

"See you tomorrow, hun," Isla said as they turned back to their phones.

As I walked home with the bread tucked under my arm, I realised something. I made new friends.

Dear Sunita,

I hope you're devouring pastries and enjoying the French sunshine. Think of me in drizzly Scotland with my sweet Granny who, bless her heart, insists on cooking me rice for every single meal. It's either boiled to mush or so undercooked it crunches between my teeth. Her desserts are pretty good though. I can't tell you anything about Grandad because he hasn't said a single word to me since I arrived. Mum said he's a bit on the quiet side, but he literally doesn't say a word.

Also, I made some new friends this week! They are a year older than me but they like the fact that I'm from London (they assumed, and I didn't correct them) and that I have an exotic name. They are no substitute for you, Dawn and May. I miss you all so much it hurts.

Lots of love,

G x

CHAPTER FIVE

SUNITA

When the white postcard arrived at the chateau, I didn't expect it to be from Gifty. For a start, the front was totally blank apart from the address. Where was the illustration? Gifty couldn't write a shopping list without some sort of drawing or sketch, so why was my postcard illustration free?

She was clearly too busy having fun with her new Scottish friends. Sigh. That thought stung a little, but I tried to be happy for her. I was glad that one of us was having fun this summer.

I was two days into my holiday at Chateau des Bores (okay, not exactly its real name) and I felt like I was in a morgue. Everyone seemed content with reading by the pool all day. No music, no TV, and no talking unless it was about what we were having for dinner.

Let's get the good stuff out of the way. The chateau is extremely Instagrammable, not that I'm into that sort of thing. With its stone walls and balconies, it looks like the sort of place that belongs in a live-action version of *Beauty & The Beast*. I must say that all this beauty is wasted on me. Gifty would be so inspired by the view of rolling lavender fields in the distance, Dawn could act out a Shakespeare scene from the balcony, and May would lose herself in a romance novel. If they were here, I'd be having so much fun.

Mum seemed to think that having people my own age around would counteract the numbing boredom, but Bryan's kids are like mini-adults. Olivia is supposedly the same age as me but talks and acts like she has a mortgage. Jack is around the same age as Anand and they are getting on like a house on fire, which is weird because Anand never gets on with anyone. Apparently, they're both into the same weirdo French philosopher and they're swapping books like normal boys swap Pokemon cards.

Mum and Bryan are annoyingly loved up. I guess it's nice to see her happy after the divorce, but does she have to mention him at every single opportunity?

You'd never guess that Mum is a partner at her law firm, the way she giggled at his jokes over dinner. It was so undignified.

Speaking of undignified, I must admit that I wasn't the most sensible person at dinner. On our first night, we walked to the village square and ate at the fanciest restaurant there. Olivia and Jack were allowed to have a small glass of wine with their dinner! Apparently, the drinking age is much lower in France. I insisted on having a splash of wine too and Mum didn't stop me because she wanted to appear cool in front of her potential new step-kids (note to self: take advantage of this at every opportunity). Olivia said the wine had notes of blackberry and chocolate, which made it sound delicious.

The thing is, no one warned me that wine is disgusting. I thought the deep red wine would taste like extra-strong Ribena but it tasted like a slightly fruity wet dog. Obviously I gagged and spat it out, making a massive stain on the white tablecloth, and everyone in the entire village square turned to look. Even the old men playing boules and smoking on the benches opposite.

"Oh dear," Bryan said like he was talking to a toddler.

"First time drinking *le vin*?"

"No! I just had a fly . . . in my throat," I said, coughing. "I think it flew out."

Everyone ignored me for the rest of the dinner which I was quite happy with because then I couldn't embarrass myself further. I drank my apple juice and kept to myself.

Of course, Olivia managed to enjoy her wine. Not only that, she ordered from the menu in French so perfect that the waiter asked her if she was Parisian. She tossed her wavy chestnut hair and giggled, insisting that she was "les Anglais". It's so unfair. I could totally order my meal in French if I studied that instead of German at school. But if I went around asking for "die Speisekarte" (that's the German word for menu . . . I think) then everyone would look at me funny.

I didn't want to annoy the waiter anymore by asking for an English translation, so I ordered the only thing I recognised: a hamburger with 'frites'.

Can you believe that Mum rolled her eyes?! "Come on Sunita, you're in France! Order something more adventurous than that."

"I recommend the steak tartare. It's a *classique*,"

Olivia said, pronouncing the last word in her fanciest French accent. It was like she was going out of her way to sound like a teacher.

"Waiter, your finest steak tartare!" I said, clicking my fingers. It was meant to be a joke, but the waiter just glared at me and no one in my family laughed, not even a sympathy chuckle from Mum. Did everyone lose their sense of humour at the airport or what?

Then my food arrived.

"Yuck!" I blurted out. "Can you guys see this?"

The waiter must have really hated me because he presented me with a plate of totally raw meat with an egg yolk sitting on top. Not a fried egg or a poached egg but a completely raw egg. I wanted to hurl.

"Mum, do you reckon we can sue the restaurant? They should be shut down!" I said.

Then I realised that I was the only one who was shocked.

"That looks like an exquisite steak tartare to me," Bryan said.

"It's meant to be raw, genius," Anand said while digging into his perfect roast chicken.

"Oh, didn't you know steak tartare was raw, sweetheart?" Mum asked.

How was I related to these traitors?

Olivia's face was the perfect picture of shock, her mouth forming an 'O' of surprise.

"Sunita, I am so sorry! I thought everyone knew steak tartare was raw," Olivia said.

I silently seethed.

"Please, allow me to swap plates," she said. As tasty as her meal of (cooked) duck breast looked, I didn't want her to have the satisfaction. Also, eating the steak tartare was an opportunity to show that I was just as mature as she was.

"No, it's fine," I said through gritted teeth. "I actually like my eggs cold and raw."

"Suit yourself," Olivia said and returned to her conversation with Mum about whether or not she should continue with Latin at A-Level.

I prodded the wet raw steak around my plate, wishing I'd stuck to my guns and ordered a hamburger. I couldn't help but look enviously at everyone else's food. If steak tartare was so "exquisite" and such a "*classique*" then why did no one else order it?

We finished the meal with everyone insisting they were too full for dessert (I was ravenous but whatever) and we walked back to the chateau. I lagged behind slightly to tie my shoelaces and saw everyone walking together: Mum and Bryan holding hands while Anand, Jack and Olivia laughed amongst themselves (probably about me). They looked like the perfect blended family, all sophisticated and sensible. And there was me on the outskirts.

I remembered what the girls and I talked about at Gifty's sleepover. Maybe I could do with growing up a little, if only so I don't spend the entire summer holiday like a pariah in my own family. Also, there was that nagging fear that my friends might grow up without me this summer. It was one thing to feel like an outcast here on holiday, but what if I got back to school and they were more grown-up than me too? I'd be totally alone in Year Ten.

I couldn't let that happen.

*

The next morning, I headed down to the breakfast table with a new intention. This was the summer I was going to show everyone I could be mature and sophisticated. I might not be poshos like Olivia and Jack, but I could act just as grown-up.

I began Operation Grown-up by ignoring the

Nutella and Frosties that I asked Mum to buy. Instead, I copied everyone else and had muesli with yogurt and a peach. I also had coffee instead of my usual apple juice. Is it any wonder that grown-ups are grumpy? Starting the day with rabbit food is enough to put anyone in a bad mood.

"I didn't know you liked coffee so much, Sunny," Mum said as I poured myself my second cup. I could get used to this, especially with half a cup of milk and three sugars in the mug.

"Are you kidding? I can't start my day without it!" I said, trying to stop my hands from shaking. It turned out that coffee gave me the jitters.

"A girl after my own heart," Bryan said approvingly. I was surprised by how much I liked hearing that.

As everyone discussed what they would do for dinner tonight, I was struck by an idea.

"How about I cook dinner tonight?" I interrupted.

"I don't think they sell chicken nuggets in Provence," Anand said sarcastically.

"I should think not," I huffed. "I was thinking of doing something more authentic."

". . . Like?" he asked.

Typical. This is the most Anand has talked to me in

weeks and it's to publicly embarrass me. What was his problem?

I shrugged Frenchly. "Oh, you know. I thought I'd visit the market and see what's on offer."

"I think it sounds like a wonderful idea, darling," Mum said.

"Me too!" Olivia said. "I can do dessert, if you like? I've been dying to try out the skills I picked up on the patisserie course Daddy got me for Christmas."

"Sounds just divine, Olivia," I said in my sweetest voice.

I had no idea what I was going to cook or how I was going to cook it. But I did know one thing: it had to beat Olivia's dessert.

If I was going to the market, I was going to go all-out and embrace the Frenchness of the situation. I borrowed a bike with a cute basket on the front and dug out the only dress I owned, a pink satin slip dress that Mum had made me wear to my cousin's birthday party. I got as far as the chateau's drive before realising that cycling in a maxi dress was impossible, so I ditched the dress in favour of denim shorts and a t-shirt.

As I cycled down the winding lane that led to

the village square, I felt for the first time like I was enjoying this holiday. I stopped to take photos of the lavender fields and mountains in the distance. When I eventually found somewhere with Wi-Fi, I would pop them in the group chat with my friends. I even took a selfie and resisted the urge to do a funny face or stick my tongue out. This was growth!

I made it to the village square, which was now transformed into a bustling market. I wheeled my bike through the crowds peering at the market stalls. On closer inspection there didn't seem to be much in the way of food. If I wanted turquoise earrings, bath salts or handmade lavender soap then I'd come to the right place, though.

I began to panic. There were no supermarkets in the village square. Where on earth was I going to get food? Then I spotted it: a little shop a few doors down from the restaurant we went to last night. The sign above it said BOUCHERIE and dead animals hung in the window. Perfect.

I wheeled my bike towards it like it was an oasis in the dessert. I parked the bike outside and stepped into the air-conditioned butchers. I was dazzled by the amount of meat on display.

The butcher said something to me gruffly in French. I recognised "Bonjour mademoiselle," but that was about it.

I panicked. What did I even want to buy? Annoying as he was, Anand did sort of have a point. I'd never cooked anything more complex than chicken nuggets before.

I recognised a pile of chicken breasts towards the back of the glass display case. They looked less intimidating than the headless birds and the unidentifiable bits of beef surrounding them. I could manage cooking those.

"Excuse me, Sir, I will have SIX chicken breasts," I said very slowly and carefully.

But the butcher still looked at me blankly. He didn't understand a word of English. I pointed to the meat and held up six fingers, but he thought I was pointing at the meat next to them (something that looked like a skinned rabbit, yuck) and began to stuff those into a plastic bag.

"No!" I yelled. That he understood.

He replied by muttering something under his breath. I didn't need French lessons to know that he was not happy with me.

"Chicken breast. Breast!" I yelled. "Y'know, like this," I said, doing my finest chicken impression (tucking my hands under my armpits, flapping them like wings and squawking. Obvs).

All those sleepovers playing charades had paid off. It seemed to work!

"Ah," the butcher said and reached for one of the scary headless chickens laying in the fridge.

"No, breast!" I said. And before I could stop myself, I pointed at my chest. Over and over again.

The butcher looked more confused than ever. How hard was it to understand I wanted six chicken boobs?!

"*Excuse-moi*, Miss?" An accented voice said behind me. Lord knows how long he'd been standing there trying to get my attention. I'd been too far into my chicken impression to hear anything.

I turned around to see the cutest guy I had ever seen. And I was clutching both my boobs and squawking like a hen.

"You are trying to order six chicken breasts, *non*?" he asked.

All I could do was nod. I was mesmerised. He had eyes so green that May would've written poetry about them.

Mystery guy turned to the butcher and spoke in a quick burst of perfect French (because he was French, duh) and the butcher nodded with relief. No doubt he was happy to talk to a sensible person. He handed me a package of meat wrapped in paper and I handed over a fistful of Euros.

I bet Olivia wouldn't have done a chicken impression in order to buy some meat. She would have asked for the chicken breasts in flawless French and asked the butcher for his life story too, no doubt.

The second worst thing about this humiliation was that I had no one to share it with. I couldn't spin it into a funny story and tell it to everyone over dinner because it would confirm that I was a Grade A fool. And I couldn't tell the girls because my stupid phone doesn't work in this stupid village, and I could only tell May (and possibly Dawn) anyway. I needed the sort of comfort that comes from telling your besties exactly how you messed up, so it becomes less of a big deal. Instead, I'll have to deal with the mental image of my squawking chicken impression popping up in my head for the rest of my life.

Maybe Gifty was right. I have to grow up.

"*Merci*," I mumbled to the butcher and to the painfully hot guy. I could at least manage to say thanks in French without fluffing it.

"You are welcome," Hot Guy said while smiling. "I am only sorry that the butcher did not understand your chicken interpretation."

"Thank you!" I said. "I'm glad someone got it."

The butcher's began to fill up with customers so I went to my bike outside. Hot Guy followed.

Was this really happening? Was this devastatingly beautiful boy making conversation with *moi*?

He leaned against a wall, his perfectly white t-shirt reflecting the sun's glare. "Are you staying in the village also?" he asked.

I explained that I was in the chateau up the hill for the next three weeks with my family (and none of my friends). When I said that, his face lit up.

"Ah! We are neighbours. My parents are on holiday in the chateau next door. Though it is not as grand as yours . . ."

"Sweet!" I said. "My name is Sunita."

"Zoo-nee-ta?" He repeated my name in the Frenchiest way possible and it was so cute I wanted to vomit. "I am Thibault."

I wheeled my bike up the windy hill and Thibault walked alongside me. The more we chatted, the more I relaxed. Thibault was friendly and chatty, nothing like most of the boys in our school. By the time we reached the chateau, I didn't care that I was a sweaty mess.

"I am just over there," he said, pointing to a smaller but charming chateau in the distance. "I am staying with my grandparents. They are sweet but they go to sleep at nine," he chuckled.

Was that . . . a hint?

"I'd invite you to dinner tonight, but I only have six chicken breasts," I blurted out.

Thibault shrugged. "Thank you, Sunita. Maybe another time, *non*?"

He waved goodbye and sauntered off all cool, calm, and collected, in his perfect t-shirt and perfect light blue jeans. Even the teenage boys here know how to dress.

I watched him until he disappeared up the road. And then I realised I had a bag full of fresh meat and standing in the midday sun wasn't going to do it any favours.

Dear Gifty,

Your gran's mushy rice sounds like a meal worthy of royalty compared to the rubbish I made everyone for dinner a few nights ago. It turns out you can both burn and undercook chicken breast at the same time, who knew?! Six chickens died in vain. Or three. I can never remember how many breasts chickens have.

Luckily Olivia made an apple tart, so we didn't go hungry. As well as being super smart and super witty she's also a super good chef. Mum and Anand love her. I can't stand her.

This holiday hasn't been a complete waste of time, though. I met a cute boy! He lives next door and his name is Thibault. Our chateau has a balcony (fancy, right?!) and I keep waiting there in the hopes he'll walk past and I can casually wave at him. No luck so far.

I am missing you and the girls too. There are so many funny stories I want to tell you but I can't because they don't translate well to a postcard. So please accept my stickman drawing of the incident where I impersonated a chicken and a boob in the butcher's.

Missing u,

S x

CHAPTER SIX

DAWN

I was ten days into life at Bright Stars Academy and, so far, I'd managed to evade every singing lesson. It was too easy: all I did was go to Madame Pearl's class just as she was doing the register, then slip out again as soon as she was done. Luckily there are two other Black girls with braids in that class and I am 99% certain Madame Pearl thinks we are the same person. I could be wrong, but I don't hang around long enough to find out.

The downside of this is that I am always a few minutes late to Fletcher's class (and he always cuts me a mean side-eye) but it's a small price to pay. What's really bothering me, though, is lying to Mum. Like when she called yesterday.

75

"Did you see that there's a steel band performing in the Showcase Extravaganza?" she asked.

It was the first thing she mentioned, after checking I was wearing my silk scarf at night (yes, but it always slipped off) and if I was eating green vegetables every day (sure – the lettuce in my cheeseburger counts, right?).

"You mean the Extras? We call it the Extras for short. And how did you know about the program already?" I didn't even know about the program already. Mum must be watching the website like a hawk.

"You should volunteer to sing one of Dad's songs!" Mum said, like the idea had only just hit her. She'd probably been plotting it since I arrived. "Get some friends from your singing class together to play back-up. I think he'd love that if he was here."

I froze. If Mum could have seen me over the phone, she'd have known that something was very wrong. Because I was one week into being at Bright Stars Academy and I had experienced approximately fifteen minutes of singing lessons.

Let me explain.

Despite our teacher, Fletcher, being something of a dragon, I am totally in love with my musical class.

It's an intensive course so it takes up most of the day, meaning it clashes directly with my singing course. I haven't technically registered for Musicals L2 but, as Fletcher has a lax approach to paperwork (he hasn't completed the register once – lucky or what?!), no one has noticed. This is partly thanks to my flagrant lie-telling. The course requires that you have completed at least one musical course in the past, either here or at another school. Luckily, no one seems to know or care that there is a wonderful little theatre school in Kent (lie) that I have attended every summer for the past three years (also a lie).

Honestly, I am so happy my friends aren't here to see me spout porky after porky. Basically the only thing I've been honest about is my name. Maybe I'm taking this reinvention thing a little too far?

"Dawn? Are you there, sweetness?" Mum asked. "I think the line froze."

"Sorry Mum, the reception isn't great in this building," I said (another lie!). "I'll call you back tonight."

Lying to Mum made me feel so guilty. But what choice did I have? It was only temporary anyway. I'd make it to a singing lesson eventually. And I really was going to think about joining the Extras to sing one of Dad's songs.

I hung up and my new friend Dante waved me over to our little group. It's super easy to make friends in this class because everyone is basically in the same boat as you: we've all left our real friends behind for the summer, and we all share the same passion for films where people spontaneously burst into song.

Dante was Jamaican, too! They live in South London but take the bus all the way into the West End every morning for musical theatre class. If Dante has parents who want them to do something else with their summer, they don't show it. In fact, I don't think Dante would do anything they didn't want to do. They are in their element in Musicals L2.

Don't get me wrong. Sunita, May, and Gifty are my ride-or-dies. But there is something incredible about joining a friendship circle where everyone greets you with the opening lyrics to *Good Morning Baltimore* (*Hairspray*, 1988). I once tried to get my friends to watch *Hairspray* at a sleepover and, apart from a shared appreciation of the main lead's hotness, they didn't get into it at all.

"Babes, are you coming with us to Subway?" Dante

asked after my phone call with Mum cut out.

They and Haniyah, another friend I'd made on the course, lingered by the doorway. Even though they were a year older than me, both Dante and Haniyah came up to me after my first class and took me under their wing. And thank goodness they did – I didn't know where anything was in the studio, and I was too terrified of Fletcher to ask.

I was going to head to my singing lesson but getting an overpriced sandwich with my new friends sounded way more appealing.

"Sure!" I said. I'd get round to the singing lessons. Besides, Mum would be happy to see I was making new friends. En route to Oxford Circus I took a moment to take in, well, the moment. Here I was, walking in the world's greatest city with two people who would have got nothing but stares back home in Kent. I'll never forget the time I persuaded Mum to let me have some purple hair in my box braids; the lady at the till in the Co-Op stared so hard she forgot to scan my Kinder Egg.

Dante, with their shaved head, meticulously groomed goatee, and exquisite eyeshadow, looked like a supermodel (and walked like one too). While

Haniyah's perfectly round face was framed by a black hijab and accentuated with flawless eyelash extensions that Mum would never let me have before I turned sixteen. Back home, they would've stopped traffic. But here in London, no one even looked up. It felt so freeing.

As we zoomed towards Oxford Street (why do Londoners walk so fast?), we talked about our class's performance for the Extras. It was just three weeks away.

"Yes, the entire academy takes part in the Extras. But everyone knows that it's Fletcher's show," Dante said breezily, as they sashayed down the street.

"Yeah! I mean, don't get me wrong, the other classes have talent," Haniyah said. "But everyone comes for the musical numbers."

This year we were performing hit tunes from Fletcher's version of the classic musical *West Side Story*. Auditions had started before the term began (if I'd actually signed up to be in this class, I'd have known that) so I was in the chorus. To be honest, it was a relief. If I had a big role in the musical there was no way I'd be able to do singing lessons. Not that I'd done any so far, but still.

Dante and Haniyah, on the other hand, had real roles. Dante was playing Bernardo, one of the leads, and Haniyah was a member of the Shark gang.

"I love *West Side Story*. We watch it every Boxing Day. Mum isn't into musicals, but she tolerates it for me," I said.

"You're lucky, man," Haniyah said. "My family is Somali but Mum makes us all watch these awful Turkish soap operas. If you think I'm dramatic you should see these lot."

Dante gasped dramatically. "Wait. Not into musicals?! That doesn't compute. My mum and I adore them. Without her Judy Garland obsession, I wouldn't be here."

We approached the sandwich shop and joined the queue. "My mum's obsessed with music but it has to be a) Jamaican and b) from the eighties or older," I said.

Dante rolled their eyes. "I hear you. Sounds exactly like my dad. I tried to broaden his horizons with some Doja Cat but he wasn't having any of it."

We ordered our sandwiches (remembering my conversation with Mum earlier, I even had a bit of cucumber in my tuna mayo sub) and squeezed into a table in the corner.

"So, are you nervous about the Extras?" I asked.

"Not me," Haniyah said. "I don't even have any speaking lines. All I do is dance and scowl from time to time."

Dante shrugged. "I don't really get nervous until the last minute," they said. "Then when I'm on stage, I forget all about it. It's just like I'm back home forcing my older brother and sister to watch me perform with a hairbrush mic. Why, are you?"

I *was* nervous, but not for the reasons they were expecting. Should I own up? I couldn't tell my friends back home. May was clearly too busy to bother updating the half-empty group chat. In fact, I hadn't had a single postcard yet, so I assumed they all must be having the times of their lives. So, I had no one else to talk to apart from Dante and Haniyah.

Haniyah looked up at me with concerned eyes. "Oh, babe, stage fright is only natural. It'll pass, I promise."

"It's not the stage fright," I said. Then I took a deep breath and explained. I told them that I was never meant to be in Fletcher's class at all, and that I'd missed every singing class so far.

Dante and Haniyah stared at me. Then they stared

at each other and broke into smiles.

"Sis . . . is that it?" Dante said. "You looked like you were about to confess something major."

"Right?" Haniyah said, laughing. "I thought you were gonna say something big. Like, you're actually twenty-five and pretending to be a teenager."

"Yeah!" Dante said. "Or you're an undercover cop gathering intel on Fletcher, who is on the run for being an international diamond smuggler, and—"

"Woah! You lot are being way too dramatic," I said. But their jokes were making me feel better about the whole situation.

"Obviously. We're theatre kids, innit," Dante said, returning to their chicken salad.

"So, you don't think I'm a bad person?" I asked.

"What, because you swapped dry vocal lessons for the sickest class in the entire school? We don't blame you at all," Haniyah said.

"I had Madame Pearl's class last summer. The woman constantly misgendered me and said my eyeshadow was a distraction," Dante said. "Fletcher may be tough but he's good at his job. You're much better off with him."

I put down my uneaten sandwich. I really appreciated their efforts to make me feel better, but it wasn't working for some reason. Maybe because it wasn't Madame Pearl's feelings I was worrying about hurting.

"The thing is, my mum really wanted me to take singing lessons. She and my dad had a lovers' rock band back in the nineties and they always dreamt of me reviving it. I think that's why she sent me here," I said.

"I don't get it. Why do they need you? Why can't they follow their own dream?" Haniyah asked.

"Because Dad died when I was little. Then Mum got a proper job and didn't have time to raise me, work and keep up her musical career," I said.

The table fell silent. Had I ruined the mood by telling them about Dad?

Dante reached over to squeeze my hand. "I'm really sorry to hear that, Dawn. But you can't live your life for someone else. Even if they didn't get the chance to live theirs."

"That sounds really rough for you and your mum," Haniyah said gently. "I also think you shouldn't feel guilty about wanting to live your life on your own terms."

They didn't understand. It wasn't their fault. Neither

of them had experienced the loss of a parent, so how could they?

I shrugged. "It's no big deal. Mum suggested that I sing one of his old songs in the Extras. Reckon it's too late to sign up?"

"Let's check when we get back to the academy," Dante said.

Dear Sunita,

It's official: your girl is a musical theatre KWEEN!
Well, not quite. I am an understudy to a super
important character in our academy's musical
production. I will only take the role if the actress
can't make it on stage for whatever reason,
but still at least I'm in the chorus! It's my first
musical role ever (and no, I don't count the Year
One Christmas Nativity where I played Angel
No. 7).

I know you're probably having too much fun
eating truffles by the pool, but the Showcase
Extravaganza is on the last Saturday of
August and I'd love to see your face in the
audience. Consider this your official invite (I
have also emailed you the full details on the
off chance you get some wi-fi - I don't trust
snail mail).

Write back soon! I haven't had any postcards
yet and I can't wait to hear from you guys.

Big hugs, D x

CHAPTER SEVEN

MAY

I had the hard part down: I had decided on an idea for a business venture. Then I spent all night watching YouTube videos about start-ups with my headphones on. Jenny was also up all night on her phone, but we had a gentlemen's agreement: we both pretended we were asleep and never mentioned it. Mum hated that we had phones and threatened to turn off the Wi-Fi at night, but Dad liked to unwind from a long night at the takeaway with his Sudoko app and he always forgot.

Andy was getting ready for work. I set my alarm early so I could catch him before he left for his call centre summer job (yet another reason why Mum and Dad believe his History degree was a failure –

why wasn't he working in a museum or something?). I had some serious guilt-tripping to do.

I asked him for a small cash investment in my summer business, and he insisted he didn't have any spare. Lies. He had an office job! Of course he had some money knocking about.

"I only need twenty pounds. That's nothing to you, but to me it's an entire shift at the takeaway," I said, blocking the staircase so he couldn't move past me.

"Listen, May, I would love to help you out with your summer project. But I'm literally broke until I get paid from this job," Andy sighed.

"It's not fair that you've taken my room for the summer!" I pouted dramatically.

Sometimes, you just have to pull the little sister card. I hate it when Jenny does it, but this was in aid of a good cause.

"Take it up with Mum and Dad," Andy said.

"Some of us are trying to sleep!" Dad yelled from their bedroom. He probably only got to bed a few hours earlier (he really was quite addicted to Sudoku).

"Okay, fine," Andy hissed quietly. "I've got £17.50 in my wallet. Will that be enough for your little business?"

I squealed silently. "Yes! It's plenty. Thanks, bro."

He tipped the contents of his wallet into my open hands. My first investor!

"I'll pay you back with double interest. Triple!" I whispered.

Andy smiled. "What will your shareholders have to say about that?" He tiptoed down the stairs and left for work, shutting the front door behind him so it didn't wake up the rest of the house.

It was early, but I was too excited to go back to bed. I had work to do.

I combined my initial investment from Andy with the dregs of my Chinese New Year money and went shopping. I cursed the fact that my birthday wasn't sooner. It was only three weeks away, but I needed the birthday money now!

Jenny insisted on tagging along on my trip to the local shops and I didn't mind. I thought she'd at least help carry the bags, but she insisted she needed her hands free so she could play on her Nintendo Switch and walk at the same time.

"I don't know why you bought all this flour and sugar," Jenny said as I unpacked the shopping. She sat on the kitchen counter and watched me do all the work, as usual.

"They're kind of an essential ingredient in chocolate brownies," I muttered.

"It's just that we have all of this stuff in the takeaway storeroom," Jenny said. "Mum and Dad bought massive bags of flour on their last supply shop. I remember because one of the bags split and made a mess in the car boot."

She can't be serious.

"And you didn't think to mention this before I spent half my money on baking ingredients?" I spluttered.

Jenny shrugged. "You never asked."

I wanted to scream.

"Okay, Jenny. I am asking now. If you see me about to spend a heap of cash on anything we already stock in the takeaway, will you tell me beforehand?"

Jenny folded her arms. "What's in it for me?"

"A delicious chocolate brownie. No, make that two!" I said.

Jenny tipped her head back and laughed. "Is that what you promise all your investors?" She noted the confused look on my face. "You're not the only one who listens to business stuff. Dad plays his podcasts in the car on long drives, you know."

Now this was a side to Jenny I'd never seen before. Maybe I'd underestimated her?

"What are your terms?" I asked.

"I want a ten percent cut of your profits. In exchange, I'll be your assistant. I'll help you with the shopping, take videos for TikTok, that sort of thing. Just don't ask me to do the washing up. I'm above that sort of thing," Jenny said. "And most importantly, I'll help you keep it secret from Mum and Dad until the time is right."

"But they'd be happy to see me start my own business. They seemed thrilled that lemonade girl did something," I said.

Jenny rolled her eyes. "Are you kidding? If Mum and Dad knew we were baking instead of doing homework they'd hit the roof. Look at how much stick they give Andy, and he's even more of a nerd than you."

"Well, I was going to do homework too," I said. I didn't let on that I'd done all my homework in one frenzied rush the first three days of the summer holidays. It had helped me to forget that my friends were away for the summer . . . but then I was sad I'd run out of homework.

Wow, I really was a nerd.

"It's a deal!" I said. Not because I particularly needed the help, but because it was better to have Jenny on my side than against me.

By the end of the day, we had a business name, a TikTok account and a flyer design. The entire day flew by. I had no idea it would be this much fun to make something! I wonder if this is the same thrill Gifty gets when she creates Teletubbies costumes, or what Dawn feels when she is up on stage?

I was weirdly relieved that my friends weren't around for this. It felt like less pressure. If the business tanked, they wouldn't be around to see it.

"Now all we need is some brownies," Jenny said. "I will help, but only if I'm allowed to lick the bowl."

"Before we make the brownies, we need customers," I said. "Let's make lists of who we know and go from there."

My list was kind of short. I knew three people, but none of them were in town. Sigh.

"Well, we have lots of neighbours who might be interested," I said. "Apart from the one two doors down who always complains whenever Mum fries chillies. Then there's Gifty's parents, Dawn's mum, and Lucas."

Jenny snorted. "Wow. Is that it? I have way more than you!"

She rattled off a list that included everyone in her primary school class, her Netball team, and some people I'd never even heard of.

Do you know how crushing it is when your eleven-year-old sister has a bigger social circle than you?

I gulped. "Great. Lots of potential customers."

"Yep. I'll start texting, you start baking," Jenny said.

*

The next day, I started my shift at the takeaway with a spring in my step. It was a Friday night which meant all hands on deck, so I helped Lucas out behind the counter. It was one of the few times a longer shift was bearable, when we got to work together. Lucas did hilarious impressions of the customers (especially the ones swinging by after the pub), and I had an uncanny knack for guessing someone's order the minute they stepped into the takeaway.

But that's not why I was happy. I'd sold my first batch of brownies! I must admit that Jenny is quite the saleswoman. She went from door to door and managed to sweet-talk a neighbour into ordering several trays for her barbecue tomorrow. We spent the afternoon baking, and I wrapped them up safely for hand-delivery tomorrow. Even better, I made back Andy's investment twice over! I could pay him back with interest and still have money left to put into the business. Maybe I'd treat myself to a special Girl Boss notebook?

Even Lucas noticed something was different.

"Why are you suddenly so excited to start work? Did you get a pay rise or something?" he asked.

I laughed. "A pay rise? Have you met my Dad? Every day he reminds me I'm lucky to be getting paid at all."

"So what's going on then? I could use some good news before the orders come pouring in and we get too busy to chat."

I told him about the brownies business, and he was even more excited than I was. He even placed an order for his Mum's hall party next weekend.

"I'll pay you in jollof rice, is that alright?" he asked.

"Er, sorry Lucas but—"

"Kidding! I'll pay you in cold hard cash, you ruthless capitalist. Give me your number and I'll send you more details," he said, pulling out his phone.

Just then a bunch of girls came in to the takeaway. I recognised a couple of them from my school, but they clearly all knew Lucas, judging by the way they looked him up and down. Also, why did all five of them need to come in? Only one of them was ordering food and even then it was a single cone of chips.

Then it hit me. They weren't here for the chips; they were here for Lucas. Chip Cone Girl giggled deliriously when he asked her if she wanted salt and vinegar.

Weird. Why would they be interested in Lucas? I mean, I knew Jenny had a thing for him because she couldn't say a word in front of him without blushing wildly. It was about the only time she was quiet. But these girls looked older than me. Why were they drooling over him like *he* was a cone of chips?

"What was going on there?" I asked, as soon as the girls finally left.

Lucas grinned. "Dunno what you're talking about, May."

"Those girls were all over you! It was so weird."

"Weird that some girls might be into me? I look a bit different outside my apron, you know," he said.

Then he winked at me. A funny thing happened.

I didn't burst out laughing or tease him for doing something so corny.

I blushed. Hard.

Luckily, he didn't notice because a delivery guy burst through the door to collect a giant order. But for the rest of the shift, I couldn't help but wonder what Lucas did look like outside of his apron.

The next morning, I was too excited to stay in bed. Today was the day of my first brownie delivery! While Mum and Dad snoozed, I made Jenny and I breakfast, and we planned our morning.

"I've been thinking. The brownies are delicious, but they looked a bit plain" Jenny said, munching on her buttered toast. "You need a way to stand out."

"What, like with icing? I didn't get any from the supermarket," I said.

Which was annoying because Jenny had a good point. One of my business YouTube videos said that having a USP (unique selling proposition) was essential. What was mine?

"I'm glad you agree, sis," Jenny said. "Because I made an executive decision to decorate them myself."

She saw the look on my face and wilted. "Don't get mad! They turned out really well," she said.

I immediately got up and marched to the pantry, where we'd hidden the brownies from Mum and Dad. But my irritation dissolved when I saw the decoration. Jenny had dotted the brownies with pink sugar balls in the shape of the letter M surrounded by a giant heart, then carefully re-wrapped the trays in layers of cling film to keep them fresh.

I walked back into the kitchen. "They look nice, so I forgive you. But don't mess with the product before running it by me again, okay?"

"Promise!" Jenny beamed. "But I knew you'd like them. I even took pictures and videos for TikTok, too."

We dropped off the brownies at No. 19 down the road, who paid in cash, then rewarded ourselves with ice lollies from the corner shop. We ate them in the paddling pool, cooling our feet in the small inflatable while it filled up with icy water from the hose. It was a blazing hot day, the sort of day I'd usually spend lounging in the park with the girls. I would hide under the nearest tree for shade, while they worked on their tans and overheated.

While we ate rocket lollies, I told Jenny about our next assignment: Lucas' mum's hall party next weekend. We chatted about potential new flavour combinations for the entire afternoon.

When Mum came downstairs for a cup of tea, she was pleasantly surprised to see us in the garden together. "It's so nice to see you girls getting along," she smiled.

I guess we *had* gone a whole morning without arguing, which was strange for us. Maybe it's a sign of Jenny's maturity – she's finally catching up to me. She is starting Year 7 next term, after all.

"Well, May is being nice for a change. She bought me an ice lolly!" Jenny said.

Mum smiled, before slipping away to get ready for work. Saturdays were even busier than Fridays and there would be plenty of prep-work to do.

I stared at Jenny. "What do you mean by that? I'm always nice."

"You're never here," she said, slurping on the dregs of her lolly. "And when you are here, you're always texting your friends or writing in that notebook. You totally ignore me."

"I . . ." I began a defence, but I couldn't actually argue with Jenny. When I was at home, I did try my hardest to ignore her because she could be so annoying. It's like she knew exactly what to say to wind me up.

So rather than blowing up at her, it was easier to lock myself into my room or hang out with my friends.

At least, it was . . . until Andy stole my room and my friends abandoned me for the summer.

"Well, I'm here now!" I said. "You have me all to yourself. Anyway, we should work on the business some more. Have you heard back from any more potential customers?"

Jenny shrugged, her eyes closed as she leant back in the deck chair and soaked up the sun. "Haven't checked."

"Well, don't you think you should? Time is money!"

"May, chill! It's the weekend, it's boiling hot and we're enjoying ourselves. Just . . . relax!"

Easy for her to say. She was the youngest and had precisely zero responsibilities. No part-time job and no Dad breathing down her neck about maintaining perfect Maths scores. Jenny just had a few household chores, which she treated as optional.

It drove me mad that she was so relaxed all the time. How did she manage it? I couldn't leave so much as a dirty cup in the sink without feeling guilty. I see how hard Mum and Dad work.

Suddenly I remembered why I avoided Jenny so

much at home. She just got under my skin, even if she wasn't trying.

I was about to make my excuses and leave, when I heard the door buzzer. Saved by the bell. I jumped out of the paddling pool, dried my feet, and walked to the front door.

It was the neighbour from No. 19. And she looked furious.

Dear Dawn,

It feels silly sending you a postcard when you're just one text message away, but it also feels odd texting you when the group chat is empty. I'm sure you're too busy for memes and gifs in London, anyway. Every day must be an adventure.

I can't exactly say the same here. I'm trying different ways to keep entertained (and make money) during the summer but nothing seems to be working.

Home is very much as you left it AKA too boring for words. So instead of illustrating this postcard with another shift at the takeaway, I have drawn my impression of you in London. That round thing in the sky is the London Eye and that tall spike is the Shard. Uncanny, right?!

I hope your teacher has become less of a dragon. After three whole years of Mr Jackson's Biology classes, I think you can handle him. I'm sure you've charmed him with your beautiful voice, just like you charm everyone else.

Yours Forever, M x

P.S. Do you remember Lucas, who works in the takeaway? What do you think of him?

CHAPTER EIGHT

GIFTY

It had been three days since I bumped into Isla, Megan and Skye in the village square. But I hadn't seen them since. Not because Granny kept me cooped up in the cottage. In fact, it was quite the opposite. She was always telling me to go for a walk and some fresh air, like I was a Labrador or something (to be fair, there isn't much to do here apart from walk and breathe).

But even though the girls invited me to hang out with them, I couldn't do it. My clothes suddenly seemed drab and dull compared to theirs. One of my few non-paint-covered outfits was a pair of mustard dungarees Mum had picked out for me. At home they seemed comfy and cute, but next to those girls it seemed childish. And I realised the colour was too similar to baby poo for my liking.

No, first impressions were everything. I had a real shot at making friends for the summer and I couldn't blow it. I only had one choice.

I had to go shopping.

The perfect opportunity came when Granny decided she needed to go to the Marks & Spencer in town. I tagged along because, let's be honest, even a basic shopping trip seemed like a massive adventure at this point. When Granny went to M&S, I swerved into Primark and cobbled together a few decent outfits and some make-up as quickly as I could. It completely wiped out the emergency money Dad had given me, but I couldn't think of anything more important to spend it on. As far as I could see, the only non-edible things they sold in the village were stamps and boot polish.

I also took the opportunity to finally use the internet on my phone, but the group chat with the girls was totally dead. I thought about posting a hand-waving emoji but decided against it. I guess they wanted to stick to the postcards.

"So, Gifty, have you made any friends in the

village since you arrived?" Granny asked me on the drive home.

The question surprised me. She'd talked most of the journey, and I was happy to nod along as she explained the latest plot on some radio soap drama.

"Oh. Erm, I guess I have," I said, talking about the three girls in the village square.

"You know, I don't believe I've met them. They must be visiting from elsewhere. There are quite a few holiday homes in the village and they are mighty popular in the summer," Granny said.

Who would willingly spend the summer here? I didn't say it out loud, but my face must have said it all because Granny started chuckling.

"Some people like the fresh country air and the solitude," she said. "But I see you are just like Gillian. She couldn't wait to leave either."

There was a note of sadness in Granny's voice that made me feel a bit guilty.

"It's really pretty around here. I was going to sketch the thatched roof on the cottages," I said, which was true. It just hadn't stopped raining long enough for me to stay outside.

"Well, when you do, ask your gran'da for an easel.

He used to paint all the time but now he hardly does. You can use his equipment."

"Thanks, Granny," I said.

Even though it was a sweet offer, I had no intention of following up. That would mean talking to Grandpa and he so clearly wasn't interested in doing that. So, I was taking the hint and keeping to myself.

*

The next day I dressed in my new outfit: a denim skirt, black tights, ankle boots and a black turtle-neck jumper. I looked like a moody artist because I'd decided black was the safest option. Mum never let me wear black clothes; she said it looked too "maudlin" on a child.

I guess I'm not a child any more.

There wasn't much I could do about my hair, so I slicked it back with gel into a topknot so it wasn't quite so . . . everywhere. And I applied a bit of make-up, which was easy enough. It was like painting but for my face. It didn't look quite as good as when Holly and the other Year 10 girls did their make-up, but the effect was instant: I did look older and more grown-up. I no longer looked like someone who was dressed by their mum, which was basically my end goal.

I thought about taking a selfie but decided against it. I had no one to send it to. Besides, the internet was so slow here it would probably take the rest of the summer to upload one photo.

Granny called me down for breakfast (no muesli or sugar-free cereal here – Granny believed in a cooked breakfast every day), and I sat down at the table as nonchalantly as I could.

I needn't have bothered. I might as well have cart-wheeled into the kitchen with the fuss Granny made about my new look. Even Grandpa did a double-take before returning to reading the morning news on his iPad.

"Does your mother let you wear make-up?" Granny asked, as she tipped scrambled eggs from the pan onto my plate.

"Of course," I said. Which wasn't technically a lie. It's not that I was banned from wearing make-up, I'd just never tried it.

"Lovely," Granny said. "Are you off anywhere special?"

"Just thought I'd see those girls again in the village

square," I said.

At that Granny really lit up. She was so happy at the thought of me going outside and talking to "lasses my own age" that she packed me off with a Tupperware box of homemade oat biscuits to share with my new friends.

After breakfast, I put my plan into action. I would walk to the village square and do a few circuits of the surrounding roads until I saw the girls. I had no idea if they'd be there again today, but it wasn't like I had anything better to do.

I took a slow walk to the village square. It didn't take me long to realise that my ankle boots were entirely unsuitable for the muddy bog surrounding the cottage. I didn't fare much better when I reached actual roads. The cobbled paths were slippery from the rain, and I wasn't used to walking in heels. I ended up tottering awkwardly all the way to the village square.

"This will be a funny story one day," I muttered to myself.

If I was with the girls, Sunita would've turned it into something hilarious and we'd have been falling over laughing by now. But falling over on your own is nowhere near as funny.

By the time I made it to the village square, my chic black boots were caked in thick mud and my feet were screaming. Did heeled boots always pinch at the toes? I hated to admit it, but I longed for my battered trainers with proper ankle support.

Luckily, I didn't have to circle the village square waiting for the girls to arrive. They were already there. I heard their shrieking giggles as I entered the square and saw them sitting on their unofficial bench. I cheered up immediately on hearing their laughter, which was kind of weird considering I barely knew them. I guess it reminded me of my friends.

As I walked over, they were alerted by the clopping of my heavy ankle boots and looked up from their phones.

"Oh hey, it's London Girl!" Skye said. "What happened to the hair?"

"It's Gifty," I said quietly. But I smiled to let her I know I didn't mind that she'd forgotten my name. "And I just tied it back today."

"What have you been up to?" Isla asked. "We haven't seen you in a while."

I shrugged nonchalantly. "Oh, not much. I did some shopping in town."

They burst into surprised snorts of laughter. "You went shopping *here*?" Isla said. "Why would you bother?"

Ah yes. They thought I was incredibly cool and lived in London, for some reason. It would be weird now to tell them I lived in a small town several train stops away from the capital, wouldn't it? I was too far in.

"I . . . ran out of a few things," I lied. Then I remembered the gift from Granny in my rucksack. "Would anyone like a homemade oat biscuit?"

I opened my bag and produced the small Tupperware tub.

"Ooh, yes please!" Megan said cheerfully and grabbed a biscuit.

"Not for me. I don't eat carbs after breakfast," Isla said, tossing her hair over one shoulder.

Skye followed suit, also turning down the biscuits. "I don't eat breakfast at all these days," she said boastfully.

Megan flushed pink and looked like she regretted taking one at all. Who knew that the offer of a homemade biscuit could have been so polarising?

Just as I was about to regret coming here with stupid biscuits, they scooched over on the bench and made space for me. I guess that meant I was 'in'.

The conversation turned quickly to Isla's annoying older brother, who the two other girls seemed to like. They didn't make any effort to include me in the conversation, which was fine with me, I guess. I wanted to keep my lies to a minimum, and, if they asked me about life in London, I wouldn't have a clue. I'd only been a few times and never for longer than one night. I didn't know anyone who lived there, so there wasn't any reason to go apart from the odd theatre trip for Mum. Dad used to go to stock up on Ghanaian food, but now you can get plantain and yam in Maidstone, so he stopped trekking to London.

Luckily, I was a good listener and from their conversation, I learned that they were staying here for the summer in the holiday homes on the other side of the village. Granny did a brief detour and pointed them out yesterday on the drive back from town. They were big, with balconies and decks and huge glass windows. But I preferred the quaint charm of Granny's cottage. I told her that and she seemed very happy.

But, back to the girls. They were from Edinburgh, but Isla, Megan and Skye came here every summer with their families. Isla and Megan were cousins, while Skye's family owned the summer home a few doors down.

"I don't know why we have to spend every summer in this tired old village," Isla huffed. "They don't even have a Starbucks!"

Northstone didn't have a Starbucks either, just two greasy spoons and a coffee cart outside the train station. But they didn't need to know that.

"I know, right?" Skye agreed. "I begged Ma to let us stay in Portugal another week, but she wasn't having any of it."

"Urgh, my Dad keeps on trying to get me to go hiking with the family," Isla said. "Mud and midges, can you imagine?!"

The girls made gagging faces and looked at me when I didn't react. I realised it had been about twenty minutes and I hadn't said a single word.

"If you want to talk about gross, you should smell the cows right outside our cottage. The country air smells vile!" I said.

Isla beamed at me. "We're city girls. We're not cut out for the country life. I mean, look at this village. The average age must be one-hundred-and-five!"

"Honestly, I was so pleased to see you girls because

you're the first people my own age I've seen all week. It's just been me and my granny, and she doesn't stop talking. Ever! I've basically zoned her out," I said.

The girls cackled and I was surprised. It wasn't that funny, was it? I instantly felt a pang of guilt. Granny did talk a lot, but she was very sweet and I didn't need to make fun of her like that.

"You must be bored out of your mind here," Skye said. "If we were in Edinburgh, there'd be a tonne of guys just walking about. I bet it's the same in London, right?"

I nodded. "Oh yeah. Loads."

I was secretly pleased that there weren't any guys around. I had zero track record of talking to boys outside of school. Dawn, Sunita, and May (it's so obvious that Lucas from the takeaway is into her, although she can't see it) all have more experience with them.

It wasn't that they scared me or anything. I just wasn't sure if I was really into them. Maybe it was just the boys in my school or maybe I just wasn't that into boys at all. Whatever the reason, I was in no hurry to decide. But it wasn't something I wanted to discuss with my new friends (even calling them my friends felt odd). I hadn't even discussed it with my real friends.

"I bet you have loads of hot guys queuing up to message you," Isla said, her eyes flashing. "You have this sexy exotic look going on. There's no one who looks like you in my neighbourhood."

I burst out laughing. I couldn't help it.

Me, sexy? I'd met house plants that were more seductive.

"She does!" Isla shrieked. "Show us, won't you?"

"Show you what?" I asked.

Isla looked at me like I was stupid. "The boys on your phone, duh! I want to see how London boys text."

"Oh! Erm . . . my phone doesn't work in this village," I said.

"Mine does. Sounds like an excuse to me," Skye said.

"No, really. I don't get any data at all. See," I said, showing them the zero bars on my phone screen.

They gasped like I'd showed them a dead kitten. "What a nightmare!" Megan said.

"Don't be an idiot, Megan," Isla said sharply. "If she goes quiet for a few weeks, they will think she's some mega babe with an incredible life. Treat 'em mean, keep 'em keen. That's what I say."

She said the last bit as confidently as if she'd invented the phrase herself.

Phew. I was saved by crap phone reception. If Isla scrolled through my messages, she'd see nothing but texts from Mum, Dad, and a dead group chat.

She dropped my phone on my lap. "No wonder it doesn't work. Your phone is such a brick!"

"Yeah, I'm due an upgrade," I mumbled, chucking my phone into the bottom of my rucksack.

Little did they know the struggle I'd had to get a smartphone in the first place. Mum and Dad would've been content to let me have the most basic of phones, just so they could call and check up on me when I was outside the house. But then they agreed to let me at least have a phone with a camera, when I told them I'd need it for the Photography modules in GCSE Art.

Luckily, they believed me.

The rest of the morning passed by, with us chatting and sharing our favourite memes. That was one thing we had in common at least. I held the phone as Isla persuaded us to make a silly TikTok video, and I must say, my input made it a lot better. I suggested different angles that made the video more interesting, and they seemed dead impressed by my ideas. It felt obvious to me, but I accepted their praise nonetheless. It felt like they were praising me for something genuine, for once.

It was soon the late afternoon, and I felt my tummy rumbling. I knew Granny would have a hot lunch waiting. And even though the clouds had cleared to reveal a bit of watery sun, I was still cold.

As I was about to make my excuses and leave before my noisy tummy gave me away, I noticed some activity in the square. A small van had pulled up, and a man in an anorak was unloading equipment from the back. He waved to people in the shop and around the square, and they looked pleased to see him.

He wasn't alone. A teen girl dressed in jeans and an oversized check shirt jumped out of the front seat to help him to lug the equipment out of the back. I watched them out of the corner of my eye, surprised that the girls didn't seem to care. Any sort of activity in the village seemed worthy of attention.

When the man in the van drove away, he left the girl behind with big boxes of stuff. As she unpacked the stuff, I realised what it was: tins of paint! And brushes and rollers on long handles. She looked too young to be a decorator, so what was she doing?

115

Megan noticed me staring. "That's the local handyman and his daughter. Mr Wright does all the repairs on our holiday home."

"Mr Wright was a lifesaver when our indoor pool heater stopped working," Isla said. "But his daughter's a bit weird. She follows him around like a lost puppy. And she never spoke a word."

"Yeah," Skye said. "I think she likes working with him. Imagine mucking about with plumbing and thinking it was fun!"

"It doesn't look like she's plumbing now," I said quietly, as the girl opened a tin of paint.

Isla turned to look at her. "Painting? She's such a baby," she sneered. "At least it won't matter if she ruins that ugly shirt."

The girls chuckled meanly. My hunger was a distant memory, but I still wanted to get out of there.

"I'd better get going," I said.

"Oh, so soon?" Isla pouted. "I wanted you to help me with another video. You're way better than these two."

I warmed to the compliment. "Um, okay. Same time tomorrow?"

"Sure," Isla smiled. The other two girls beamed at

me identically.

I couldn't help how good it made me feel. What can I say? I missed my friends. Having these girls as friends for the rest of the summer felt better than staying in the cottage and being alone with awful memories of Holly's party.

I walked (carefully) along the cobbles towards the road that led to the cottage. Even though pain flooded my toes as soon as I got up, I took the long way round so I could see what the girl was up to.

She poured white paint into a tray and soaked the roller. Then she lifted it up to the grey wall and, in one single movement, swiped the roller down. Slowly but surely the wall was transformed into a blank white canvas, and I was mesmerised.

Dear May,

I never thought I'd see the day where I'd actually miss our crummy little town. I miss the three buses an hour. I miss the queue for the ice cream van outside the park. I even miss the greasy spoon where the hot chocolate is always served with a skin (bleurgh).

But homesickness will do that to you. Even though Dawn and Sunita are having real holidays, it's you I envy the most.

I'm sorry this postcard doesn't come with an illustration, even though it was my idea in the first place. I'm not feeling very inspired to draw right now. Is there such a thing as artist's block? I think I have that.

Lots of love,

G x

CHAPTER NINE

SUNITA

It's official. My Mum is an opp. Because why else would she go out of her way to sabotage my relationship with Thibault?!

Okay. Maybe calling it a relationship is a slight exaggeration. It had been six days (plus three hours and fifty-two minutes, but who's counting? Not me!!) since we first met. And we hadn't talked since because I just hadn't seen him. Lord knows I tried. I've invented every possible excuse to walk past his chateau and go on random errands into the village. I even hung around the butcher's two days ago to see if he was there, but nothing!

But just as I convinced myself that I'd hallucinated him, he turned up. I was on my bi-daily bike ride to the shops when he appeared, all handsome and French. He was coming up the road from the village and the shopping bags indicated he'd already been to the shops. Damn it! If I was just twenty minutes earlier, I could have met him.

Play it cool, Sunita.

"Thibault, hi!" I said, waving frantically like a shipwrecked sailor.

I just wanted to make sure he saw me, okay?

"Oh, hey Sunita," he said and smiled slowly.

He remembered my name. He remembered my name! He didn't call me Sonia or Suzy or Sareeta (believe me, I have had them all). That means I must've made an impression.

I wheeled my bike over and was about to compliment him on his excellent bag-carrying skills when we were rudely interrupted.

"Who's your friend, Sunita?"

I turned around to see where the voice was coming from. It was Mum! She was hanging around the front door of the chateau like some creeper.

"It's no one!" I said at exactly the same time as Thibault introduced himself.

Why did he have to be so polite?

"Nice to meet you, Thibault," Mum said.

"This is my mum," I said, while silently seething. No way was I going to introduce her by name.

"That is your mother? I thought your older sister perhaps," Thibault said.

I burst out laughing, but he was serious. And Mum was absolutely charmed by it, too. She giggled *and* blushed. Honestly, she should be embarrassed. A woman of her advanced years acting like that?

"Thibault, I'm sure Sunny would love it if you joined us for dinner tonight. I've made way too much *coq au vin*," Mum said.

"*Coq* au what?!" I blurted out. "Language, Mum!"

She rolled her eyes. "It's a chicken stew, Sunita."

Thibault looked so happy to be invited. He agreed to join us later that night for dinner, then he had to take the shopping home. Which meant I didn't get to say a single word to him without Mum butting in.

And the next time he sees me, I'll be surrounded by my entire family. Plus Bryan, Olivia and Jack.

Then, another thought shot through my mind. What the heck was I going to wear?!

When he had disappeared down the road, I dashed the bike to the ground and ran back into the chateau. Mum was waiting inside the hallway looking all smug.

"So, is he the reason you've been looking mournfully up the road all week?" she asked. "He's very handsome! I thought we could eat on the balcony tonight, seeing as it's a special occasion."

When I marched up the stone stairs (honestly, this place is like a Disney castle) without saying a word, Mum asked me what the problem was.

"The problem is that you invited Thibault without asking me first!"

"I thought I was doing you a favour," she said sadly.

I paused at the top of the stairs. "What are you talking about? I can't have him here!" I spluttered.

Mum looked at me all confused. "Why not? Are you embarrassed by us?"

How can someone be that clever and clueless at the same time?!

"Because . . . because . . ."

Because everyone is this family thinks I'm a silly child. And I'm afraid they might be right. And I'm afraid that Thibault will see me next to real adults and agree with them.

But I couldn't say it to Mum. She seemed genuinely

puzzled. I knew she wouldn't get it.

"Because I have nothing to wear!" I yelled before running to my room.

That's another annoying thing about living in a chateau. The heavy wooden doors move too slowly to slam dramatically when you're in the middle of a fight.

I slumped onto the four-poster bed and sighed heavily. I really did have nothing to wear! The only date-worthy outfit I had was the pink satin dress and I stained it when I ate a particularly juicy peach.

I spent the next hour rifling through my suitcase (I still hadn't gotten around to unpacking yet – May would be so unimpressed with me) and sorted all my outfits into YES or NO piles. After ten minutes, the NO pile was a mountain and the YES pile consisted of a few pairs of earrings.

This. Was. A. Disaster. For the fiftieth time that trip, I checked my phone to see if I'd magically developed a data connection and the girls had updated the group chat.

"Come on, please! This is my darkest hour!" I pleaded to the phone. But nada.

Maybe I wasn't trying hard enough. Had I really tried to get my phone working? Like Mr Saunders said in my end-of-year school report, I could achieve great things if I stopped messing about.

Well, I wasn't messing now. *Think, Sunita, think!*

Yes, the chateau had thick walls but what if I got my phone higher? When we went on a camping trip for Duke of Edinburgh and got lost using those silly paper maps, we managed to connect our phones by going to the highest point and waving them around. It didn't help us find our way back to camp because we couldn't navigate using Google Maps either and the teachers had to send out a search party, but at least we could text them for help.

Then I saw it. The ancient-looking chest of drawers and wardrobe in the corner of the room. There was a Sunita-sized space on top of the wardrobe that was at least ten foot in the air. I gave it a good shove and it didn't budge. Perfect.

The chest of drawers was too tall for me to jump on (if only I had Dawn's height!). I stood on the bed and lunged one foot forward, stretching so I had one foot on the bed and one foot on the chest of drawers. I felt like I was doing the splits in mid-air.

"Woahhh!" I wobbled slightly, but managed to steady myself.

I was basically Simone Biles.

Now, I just had to get the other leg to the top of the drawer. My back leg was starting to ache, which made my entire body shudder. You'd think all that cycling back and forth to the shops would have given me calves of steel!

"You have got to stop skiving PE," I muttered to myself, as I felt my confidence drain with every second that passed.

I waved the phone in the air, but that made me wobble even more. And then it dawned on me.

I was stuck. For some reason I couldn't get my legs to move! I couldn't work up the nerve to step back onto the bed in case I fell and hit the stone floor. And I certainly couldn't jump forward onto the chest of drawers – it was too narrow for me to fit.

Why was I cursed with being such a doofus?

Someone knocked on the door, interrupting my self-loathing spiral.

"Sunita? It's me, Liv."

Oh no. Not her. I couldn't let her see me like this. Why couldn't it have been Anand or Mum? They already think I'm an oversized toddler anyway.

"W-what's up, Olivia?" I was trying to sound casual,

but my legs were really starting to ache.

"Meera said you needed a nice outfit for tonight? I have a few dresses you can borrow, if you like," she said.

Why did Mum have to say something to Liv?! Now she's donating her cast-offs to me like I'm a Victorian orphan.

"T-t-thanks, Liv. But I don't want to put you through any trouble," I stuttered.

"It's no trouble at all, Sunita. Daddy teases me for my heavy luggage, but I like to pack for every occasion! The trick is to roll rather than fold," she said through the door. Why was she telling me this? "I'll pop them on the bed, and you can decide if you like them."

"No!" I shrieked. She couldn't come in. I'd rather fall to the floor and split my head open. "Just . . . put them on the floor outside."

"But they'll get dusty. I'll just throw them on the bed," Olivia said.

Before I could stop her, she pushed open the wooden door and tossed the clothes on my bed.

"Oh! What *are* you doing?" Olivia asked.

I turned my head to face her. "Umm . . . stretching?"

"You really shouldn't stand on that antique furniture. It's probably as old as the chateau," she said. "Let me give you a hand."

I was in no position to turn down help. She stood next to me and held out both of her hands. I grabbed them and jumped down from the bed, landing softly (well, as softly as you can land on flagstone floors) on the ground.

"Um, thanks," I said. I felt my face flush even harder than the first time I met Thibault. "And thanks for the clothes."

"See you at dinner tonight," she said before leaving the room. "And keep whichever dresses you like; I don't wear them anymore."

I could tell she was trying not to giggle as she left the room. Is it any wonder? I'm nothing short of ridiculous. Which would be fine, maybe even endearing, if I was a little kid, but I'm not anymore.

Well, Olivia wasn't the only one who could be charming and sophisticated. And I was going to prove it.

*

By the time dinner rolled around my stomach was

127

in knots. Delicious cooking smells wound their way through the chateau, but I couldn't even think of eating. I was too stressed about the thought of impressing Thibault! Imagine, my first real date with a boy and it was in front of my entire family plus Bryan, Jake and Olivia.

At least I looked good. As much as I hated to admit it, Olivia's cast-offs were nicer than anything I'd packed. I picked a black halterneck dress with thigh splits and twisted my wavy hair into an up-do, with curly tendrils framing my face. I didn't bother much with make-up and I wasn't about to start experimenting now, but I could manage mascara and lip-gloss. Besides, I was going for the sophisticated look and that meant 'less is more'. I think?

I decided to model my new persona on the star of the old-fashioned French movie we'd watched a few days ago. The closest thing this place has to a cinema is an outdoor screening of some geriatric film once a week. It was a black-and-white French movie from the 1960s with no subtitles, but it was better than sitting in the chateau by myself. And I thought there was a chance I'd spot Thibault in the audience, and I'd be able to gaze from afar.

I didn't spot him, but it wasn't a completely wasted trip. I didn't need to understand the language to know that the female lead was a total babe who was worshipped by every guy in the film. She had this sexy mysterious thing going on and she never cracked jokes. In fact, I don't think she ever laughed unless it was when one of her many admirers got down on one knee to propose. She was the total opposite of me (as the girls tell me, my emotions are always plain as day on my face) but that was okay. I had a plan.

I swanned into dinner fifteen minutes after Thibault arrived, because I had to make an entrance. But everyone was too busy chatting, eating olives and asking Thibault questions to notice me glide in late. I cleared my throat delicately and when that didn't work, I coughed loudly (I don't recall Miss Femme Fatale having to do this in the film). But I must've coughed too loudly because Bryan looked all concerned and asked me if I needed some water, and was I coming down with something?

But then Thibault smiled at me, looking genuinely happy to see me, and I lost the ability to talk. Heck, my brain synapses may have stopped firing for a full three seconds. When I snapped back to reality,

I noticed that all the seats close to Thibault were taken (he was squeezed between Anand and Olivia, poor guy) so I had to sit at the head of the table.

Now, how was I going to get him to notice me without saying or doing much? It seemed to me that Femme Fatales were more of the silent types. I decided to keep my sunglasses on for the entire meal (see: mysterious!) and pout seductively.

The sunglasses got a bit annoying when the sun set and Mum lit candles instead of turning on the balcony lights, so I really couldn't see much of what was on my plate. But as I was eating teeny-tiny bites of chicken stew (chewing was not FF behaviour), it didn't matter much.

"Don't worry Sunita, I got apple juice just for you," Bryan said kindly.

While everyone else had wine mixed with water in chic crystal glasses, I had a plastic tumbler of juice.

"Oh, no! I *j'adore* French wine," I said.

"Mum, Sunita is talking in weird voices again," Anand muttered. "I think she has sunstroke."

"I love the English sense of humour," Thibault said, smiling.

"There's English humour and there's Sunita's

humour, which is in a world of its own," Anand said.

Suddenly I didn't care about being a Femme Fatale. I was so angry at Anand for always putting me down. I whipped off my sunglasses.

"At least I *have* a sense of humour. You're so dull that—"

"That's enough, kids," Mum said. She was trying to be all Cool Step Mum but I could tell she was getting annoyed with us.

"Just grow up," he muttered under his breath.

Why was he always so mean to me? Why did he hate me? He'd been weird ever since Dad left.

Everyone returned to their food and conversations while I silently seethed. Olivia and Thibault giggled over something in French, Jack and Anand were chatting about some dull book, while Mum and Bryan were no doubt playing footsie under the table.

I took a swig of my apple juice and sank back into the chair. So far, being a Femme Fatale was not only boring . . . it wasn't actually working. Thibault and I had barely spoken all evening, other than to compliment my outfit (he said it was *tres* Audrey Hepburn).

When it was time for dessert (some apricot cake

Olivia made – I didn't have any on principle), I'd given up entirely on ever seeing Thibault again. It was clear I wasn't impressive enough. If my own family didn't even take me seriously, why would he?

"That was delicious, Liv," Thibault said. "Don't tell my *grandmere* but you bake better than she does."

Olivia blushed and I actually didn't blame her. If someone as hot as Thibault complimented my cake, I would drop everything to start my own bakery.

"Sunita, why don't you walk our guest out?" Mum suggested. She even winked! But because Bryan had been topping up her glass with red wine all night, it wasn't the subtle move she thought it was.

I hustled Thibault into the house before he noticed.

"Thank you for a lovely evening, Sunita," he said gorgeously. "I really like your family, even though they talk a lot."

I couldn't help but smile. So, he had noticed my mysterious quietness!

"Yeah, they don't shut up," I said.

He stepped forward and my heart raced. "Do you like to 'ike?" he asked.

"Yes, I love it!" I said.

I had no idea what he meant of course, but if he

asked me if I liked badgers I would have said yes.

"*Parfait*. I will meet you here tomorrow morning," he said. "Good night."

Then he sauntered off down the road.

Dear Dawn,

I think I've hit the boy jackpot. I know you're probably surrounded by cuties in London but here in this tiny village, my options are severely limited. So, imagine my surprise when the only hot guy for miles around happens to be into me?

Well, I'm not entirely sure if he is into me. But he's the only person around here who doesn't find me annoying or childish, so that's a plus. He also invited me to an Ike (sp?) tomorrow morning (yes, I am writing this in bed). I have no idea where that is – it's probably a local coffee shop or something.

I tried and failed miserably to get Wi-Fi, sacrificing my calves in the progress. Don't ask. I miss you guys so much, but I know you're taking London by storm, and that makes me feel slightly better about being apart from you for so long.

I'm too tired to illustrate the postcard (don't tell Gifty). Instead, I will cover it in lip-gloss kisses.

Missing u!

S x

CHAPTER TEN

DAWN

It all went wrong when Haniyah decided she wanted noodles for lunch. We began taking turns to choose lunch spots (my fave was the cafeteria because it was cheap – well, cheap for London anyway) but Haniyah decided she wanted to try something new. So, she made us trek into Chinatown for some noodle soup spot she'd seen on TikTok.

Never mind that it was a blazing August day and way too hot for soup. Never mind that the place had queues down the road. Still, it was her turn, so we queued up and I got to see Chinatown for the first time. I spotted about five different foods I just had to try before I went back home (bubble tea, char sui dumplings, Korean fried chicken, roast duck and ramen), so it wasn't a waste of time.

But I was just a few bites into my (admittedly delicious; Haniyah wasn't wrong about that) soup when I caught the time: I was about fifteen minutes late for afternoon registration with Madame Pearl!

It was especially annoying because I had to leave my food behind.

"I've gotta go!" I said, picking up my stuff in a hurry. "I'll pay you back later!"

Dante sighed. "Don't worry, sis. We got you."

"Babe, you may as well finish your soup. You're already late!" Haniyah said.

But I was already on my way out the door. It was the second time this week that I'd missed registration. If it happened again, they'd phone Mum and that was one awkward conversation I didn't need to have.

I ran into the class as the lesson was mid-swing. Not a surprise seeing as it started twenty-five minutes earlier. But I must have run to the wrong class because Madame Pearl wasn't there. In her place was a younger woman leading the class.

She paused the singing and turned to me. "May I help you?" she asked sternly.

"Sorry, I missed registration. Where's Madame

Pearl's class?" I asked.

"Madame Pearl has had to take a temporary leave of absence," she said. "You would know that if you weren't," and at this point she checked her watch, "thirty minutes late to the class."

I felt the flames of embarrassment lick my face. Even worse, some of the students looked confused to see me there.

The woman picked up the register. "Name?"

"Dawn Carter," I mumbled.

"We're rehearsing the class piece for the Extras. Take your position, please."

"Yes, Miss," I said. I stared blankly at the rest of the class, who were standing in three rows.

I had no idea where I was supposed to go. I slotted myself at the end of the nearest row.

The rest of the lesson was excruciating. I had no song book and had no idea what song we were meant to be singing. The teacher, whose name was Sally, kept on stealing glances at me when we were rehearsing.

On top of that, this class was eating into my Musicals rehearsal with Fletcher. Even though I was just an understudy, he was big on the fact that we had to attend all rehearsals, just in case we had to step in at the last minute.

And I was hungry because I'd skipped lunch! The last hour of the lesson crawled by because I was an anxious, ravenous mess. At the end of the lesson, I tried to leave as quietly as possible, but Sally had other ideas.

"Dawn, I am afraid I will have to inform your parent or guardian about your lateness. It's simply unacceptable," Sally said. "What's worse is that it looked like you'd never attended a single lesson. Do you really want to be here?"

"Y-yes," I stammered. "Of course!"

"Then you will have to do much better next time," she said. "Madame Pearl may have allowed such behaviour, but I shan't."

"Understood, Miss," I said.

*

"You look bare stressed, what's going on?" Kiana said. She was in her work uniform.

I jumped when she spoke. I didn't even hear her come in. I'd been sitting in the living room, waiting for the inevitable moment when Mum rang me demanding to know why I was missing lessons.

But before I could answer Kiana, the phone started to ring. Not my phone, Auntie Pat's house phone.

"Weird. No one ever calls this line," Kiana muttered. She picked up the phone. "Hello?"

She paused. "Yes, this is Patricia Henry," Kiana said. Then she spent the next few minutes saying things like "mmm" and "goodness" and "my word!" in an extremely grown-up voice.

What was she doing?

She hung up. "You've been a bad girl, Dawn. You're in soooo much trouble," she said.

"Don't tell me that was the academy?" I groaned and hung my head. "I'm expelled, aren't I? Mum is going to be so disappointed."

Kiana burst out laughing. "What are you on about? You've been late a few times! It was just a warning," she said. "They sounded like such snobs. Talking about what a 'prestigious opportunity' you're wasting, like you're not the one paying *them*."

I slumped on the sofa and sighed. I went from feeling fear to relief to embarrassment. Kiana must've thought I was such a goody two-shoes.

"You don't get into trouble very often, do you?" Kiana asked.

I shook my head. Apart from chatting in class, my reports are pretty much flawless for behaviour. Mum always rewarded me with dinner at a restaurant of my choosing after a good report. There weren't that many restaurants to choose from in our town, but still. A meal out is a meal out!

"I don't want to stress Mum out with a bad report," I said. "She has enough on her plate as it is."

Kiana sighed. "I hear that. But you don't need to be stressed either!"

Tell that to my stomach, I thought. It was a bundle of knots.

"I can't calm down yet," I said. "I still haven't heard from Mum. Wonder why they called here first?"

Kiana shrugged. "They must have had this number down as the emergency contact. They knew Mum's name."

That did make sense. Mum was all the way in Kent, while Auntie Pat was a short bus ride from the academy. If there was an emergency, it made more sense to call here first.

"They're still gonna call Mum and she's gonna be so mad," I said to myself.

"Nah, I can't deal with this. Your stress vibes are

infecting the whole flat," Kiana said. "We're getting you out of this place."

"What? You're kicking me out?!" I panicked.

Kiana rolled her eyes. "Don't be dumb. Give me five minutes to get changed, yeah?"

The time flew by while I was staring at my phone waiting for the inevitable call from Mum. I very nearly called her to own up, just to end the torment.

Twenty minutes later, Kiana emerged from her bedroom in a cute sporty summer dress and trainers. "Don't tell me you've been staring at your phone the entire time?" she asked.

"She still hasn't called," I said.

"And she won't! Gimme that," Kiana said and, before I could stop her, she whipped my phone out of my hand. "This is staying behind."

I tried to argue with her, but she gave me the same stare Auntie Pat used.

We left the flat and walked towards Camden Market. It was nearly five o'clock, but the high street was rammed with people buying ice cream in giant waffle cones and dangling their legs over the canal. It was a sticky, hot evening, and trying to keep up with Kiana's pace made me even hotter.

"Where are you taking me?" I asked.

"Less talking, more walking," Kiana said.

We soon left the high street behind and ended up on a quieter street filled with shops and restaurants, but they looked a lot posher than Camden. Some of the restaurants had Italian names and hand-painted signs, sleek cars lined the streets and expensive-looking women walked equally expensive-looking dogs. Even the charity shops looked like fancy boutiques.

I suddenly felt conscious of my drab outfit, but Kiana stomped across the pavement like she owned the place.

Finally, we made it to a green space bordered by iron fences. I felt the sweat drip down my neck from my power-walking session with Kiana and was looking forward to sitting under a tree for shade.

As if she heard my thoughts, Kiana said, "We're not stopping yet."

Instead, we ploughed along a path then up a steep hill in the baking late-afternoon sun. If I wasn't a sweaty mess before, then the final leg finished me off.

We reached the top of the hill, and I sprawled on

the grass. "Kiana! Unless you want to carry me back home, I need a break now," I panted.

She laughed. "You are so unbelievably dramatic. We're here now, anyway. You might want to get up and turn around."

I pushed myself up and turned around. Even though I was knackered, I wanted to stay in Kiana's good books. She'd actually acknowledged my existence, and I didn't want her to regret it.

"Woah!" I said under my breath.

Kiana crossed her arms and smirked. "Reckon that was worth the trip?"

London's skyline lay before us: the Shard, St Paul's Cathedral and dozens of jagged skyscrapers piercing the clear blue sky. Each of those buildings represented thousands and thousands of people, all here in one place. The thought of one city teeming with so many lives made my head spin.

I was awestruck. "I've never seen London like this before."

Kiana sat cross-legged on the grass, and I followed suit. My calves were still aching from that uphill trek.

"Not many people do. I've lived near this park my entire life but I only started coming here a couple of years ago," Kiana said.

"I'd give anything to have this view every day," I said.

As soon as I said it, I felt guilty. Having this view every day meant that I'd live in London, and that meant leaving Mum all alone. I could never do that to her.

"I mean, not every day," I added. "Once in a while is fine. Like, during holidays and the odd weekend."

"It ain't gonna happen anyway," Kiana said. "Do you know how minted you need to be to live around here, in Primrose Hill? Those houses across from the park are worth tens of millions."

I screwed up my face. "Seriously?! Are they built with gold bricks or what?"

Kiana shrugged. "That's London! Maybe when you're a famous singer you'll be able to afford one," she teased.

I didn't want to think about Mum and Dad's dream for me right now. "Why did you start coming here?" I asked, eager to change the subject.

Kiana sighed. "I think me and Mum both drove each other a little crazy over lockdown, you know? One day we got into a fight. I left the flat and walked and walked. Then suddenly I was standing in front of the park gates. I know it sounds kinda silly . . . but it was like I was meant to find it."

I nodded along, like I related to her story, but I couldn't imagine getting into a fight with Mum or stomping out of the house in a tantrum without her knowing where I was. Anyway, leaving the house would be significantly less dramatic in our neighbourhood: there was only one park, and it was five minutes from our house.

"Ever since then, I've come here whenever I need to clear my head. The wide-open space makes me feel like I can breathe," she continued.

That I could understand. I didn't notice how cramped the city felt until I came to the park.

"Thanks for bringing me here," I said.

Kiana shrugged. "You were being dead annoying at home."

I smiled. That was the closest thing I was gonna get to 'you're welcome'.

"Yeah. Sorry about that. I just couldn't handle the thought of Mum finding out," I said.

"So, why were you skiving? It must be for something good," Kiana said.

"I wasn't skiving! I was in another class," I blurted out.

Kiana looked confused. "What, in the same academy? So why–"

"Don't ask," I sighed. "It's a long, boring story."

"I'll be the judge of that," Kiana said. "Spill."

I told her that I was skipping singing lessons to be in the Musicals class with Fletcher.

"It started out as a one-off, but now I'm an understudy so I can't back out," I said. My heart raced as I told the story, and I realised what a mess I was in.

"I don't get it. What's the issue?" Kiana asked. "Can't you explain everything to the academy and swap classes?"

"But Mum and Dad have always wanted me to sing his music. I'm meant to continue their legacy, not–"

"Do what it is you actually want to do?" Kiana interrupted.

"It's not like that. I love Dad's music," I protested.

"Okay then. If you love it so much, how come you haven't gone to see a single reggae show since you've arrived?" Kiana asked.

"I-I've been too busy!"

"I knew it!" Kiana said. "I knew from the moment Mum played that demo CD that you weren't into that music. So why are you pretending?"

My eyes filled with tears. If Kiana noticed, then she didn't say anything. "Because Mum would be so disappointed if . . ."

"So what? It's your life!"

"Wow. Harsh."

She shrugged. "I said what I said. You know what your problem is, Dawn? You're a people-pleaser."

"What's so bad about wanting to please other people?" I asked.

Kiana looked at me coolly. "I knew girls like you in school. Always saying yes to everything other people wanted from them because they're too afraid to disappoint."

That cut deep. It felt too accurate. Sunita always said I was too nice for my own good, and I always took it as a compliment. But what if it wasn't a good thing?

"Don't get upset or anything. It isn't your fault! I blame patriarchy, innit," Kiana said.

"Mum always says I'm the perfect daughter. I guess I know why," I said quietly.

Kiana laughed. "Wow! I can't even imagine Mum saying that about me."

"So, what do I do about it?" I asked. It seemed like

Kiana was the expert in doing her own thing. "Say if I was going to maybe, possibly, one day tell Mum I wanted to quit this band idea and focus on musical theatre. How do I do it?"

"You just do it! That always works for me," Kiana said brightly. "We can call Auntie Sandra right now if you want." She reached for her phone.

"No!" I yelled. "I was speaking hypothetically."

"Okay. Well, speaking hypothetically . . . you need to get used to making other people uncomfortable."

"What do you mean?"

Kiana smiled. Then she stood up, tipped her head back and screamed.

No, she *roared*.

It was a full-throttled, look-at-me-making-all-the-noise sort of scream.

I was mortified. Children playing football, couples enjoying picnics, and friends lying on the grass chatting stopped what they were doing to stare at us. It felt like it lasted for hours but, in reality, it couldn't have been more than five seconds.

"Kiana, what the hell?!" I hissed.

"Stand up," she said.

"Nope! No *way*."

"Do it. Otherwise, I'm calling your mum and telling her what you just said to me," she said.

"Go on then!" I said, calling her bluff.

Kiana got her phone out and tapped a few buttons. "It's ringing . . ."

"Okay, fine!" I said, leaping to my feet. "Hang up!"

Kiana smirked and put her phone away. "Now we're going to scream for five seconds in three . . ."

Oh god, why?

". . . two . . ."

I feel sick.

". . . one . . ."

Here goes.

"AGHHHHHHHHHHH!"

We yelled at the same time, facing each other. I screamed until my throat ached and my lungs emptied. Then we stopped and immediately burst into hysterical laughter. I laughed until I cried, holding the sides of my belly.

"Wait . . . I can't breathe!" Kiana squealed as we rolled on the grass.

Finally, we stopped laughing and caught our breath. My sides ached in the best way possible.

I looked around me. To my shock and surprise,

no one was paying any attention to us. At least not any more.

"See, Dawn? It's no big deal! The world won't end just because you used your voice," Kiana said.

"That felt amaaaaaazing," I said. "Why did it feel so good?"

"I guess it feels good to be heard," she said.

Dear Gifty,

I can't believe we haven't spoken in two whole weeks! That must be some kind of record, surely? The time has flown by. London really is as hectic as everyone says it is, and I am loving every minute of it. My schedule is packed with rehearsals (get this - I'm in the end-of-term show!) and my cousin Kiana has been showing me around London. The front of the postcard illustrates our recent trip to this incredible park where she told me I have people-pleasing tendencies. Hate to admit it, but she might have a point. Maybe that's something I can work on before starting Year Ten?

You'd love it here. Where I live in Camden feels dead creative - there's lots of cool graffiti, except here they call it 'street art'. And there's a Black hair shop just five minutes from my flat! Imagine being able to pop out for leave-in conditioner? Northstone still has a long way to go.

I hope you're surviving up in Scotland. I bet you're being spoilt rotten by your grandparents, right?

Big hugs, D x

P.S. What's haggis really like?!

CHAPTER ELEVEN

MAY

It took me a whole week, but I eventually started talking to Jenny again. It was tricky to give her the silent treatment without Mum and Dad noticing, but they didn't pick up on it. As long as I talked to her at the dinner table ("pass the soy sauce" etc) no one else suspected a thing.

I know she didn't mean to, but she had destroyed my business.

When the neighbour from No. 19 knocked on our door holding a tray of half-eaten brownies, my mind raced through the horrible reasons why she was there. Maybe I'd accidentally used table salt instead of sugar, or I'd missed a rotten egg in the batter. But no. It wasn't my fault.

No. 19 was fuming. She accused me of deliberately trying to sabotage her BBQ and even threatened to sue. I apologised and handed over what was left of her cash for a refund, then shut the door in her face as she ranted. I know it was rude, but I had to get her to stop shouting at me!

I carried the brownies into the kitchen where Jenny was waiting for me.

"I don't get it! I tasted the batch, and they were fine," I said.

"Only one way to find out," Jenny said, before cutting herself a big wedge.

"Don't eat too much! What if they are actually poisonous?"

Jenny ignored me, taking a big bite. She chewed and chewed and didn't drop to the ground in agony. That was a good sign, so I cut off a small slice and ate it myself.

It was tasty. More than tasty. It was delicious, rich and dense and chocolatey. And the pink sugar balls added a lovely crunch.

"I don't get it! These brownies are amazing," I said.

Then it hit me. My mouth flooded with white-hot heat. It must have hit Jenny too because she rushed to the fridge for milk and drank it from the bottle.

"Save me some!" I squealed, pouring the milk straight down my throat.

The flames in my mouth subsided, but my entire face tingled. A bit of something hard and crunchy lodged in my tooth. I spat it into my hand and there it was: a pink sugar ball.

I had a hunch. I picked a sugar ball off the tray of brownies and crunched it. There was that peppery heat again.

"Jenny . . . you said these were sugar balls," I said quietly.

"They are," she said. "Why?"

"Go get the jar. Now."

Jenny went to the baking cupboard and came back with an unlabelled glass jar filled with pink balls. There were loads of unlabelled jars and bottles in our kitchen because Mum recycled like she was paid to do it, so that wasn't unusual. She could tell what everything was from sight and smell alone, so she didn't need to label them.

I opened the jar and took a sniff. "Jenny, these aren't sugar balls. They're Szechuan peppercorns!"

"No way! But they're so bright and pretty," Jenny said.

"Aren't you the least bit sorry? You ruined the entire batch!" I yelled.

Jenny looked at me blankly. "Sorry. But that lady was really overreacting. She could've just picked off the peppercorns and finished the batch. Oh, well. More for us!"

I stormed out of the kitchen before I said something I really regretted. I was mortified by the mistake. Why didn't Jenny seem to care?

That was the end of my short-lived brownie business. I told Lucas about the whole thing in hushed tones (so Mum and Dad wouldn't overhear in the kitchen), but I needn't have bothered. The clanging of woks and the roar of the extraction fan meant they didn't hear anything outside of the kitchen anyway.

"You shouldn't give up so easily, May," Lucas said. "What if I double my brownie order and pay early? That should help to recoup your funds."

"Thanks, Lucas, but the whole thing is tainted now. I can't bake in peace knowing that there's a target on my back. What if the neighbour leaves a nasty review online? Or actually does sue me like she threatened?!"

Lucas laughed. "I love how dramatic you are. But all right, maybe it's time to find another business.

What ideas do you have?"

"Jenny suggested dog-walking but I'm not much of an animal person," I said. "Baking brownies is the only thing I'm good at, besides doing homework on time."

"And looking good in a hairnet!" Lucas teased.

"Shut up," I laughed. "That's hardly a marketable skill."

"You're also a really good tutor. Remember when you helped me out with my History essay about the Cold War?"

I shrugged, secretly pleased that he'd remembered. "It was nothing."

"It was *not* nothing. It really helped me out. And I bet there are loads of people who would pay for help," Lucas said. "My cousin Tunde is a Maths student at uni and he gets paid loads to coach kids through their GCSEs."

"Sounds like my dad would love him," I said.

"At least think about it. You'd do a good job," Lucas said.

As he served the first in a line of customers arriving for the lunchtime rush, I thought about his suggestion. I have to be honest – the old May would love a tutoring job. I could use all sorts of nice stationery and get to explain things to people about subjects I knew pretty well. Goodness knows I'd had enough practice helping Jenny with homework, though most of our sessions consisted of her trying to bribe me to just do it for her (a less scrupulous tutor would be rolling in gummy bears).

But the new, more grown-up May? That was the exact image I'm trying to get away from. I know I'm a nerd, and I guess Lucas does too. Shouldn't I be aiming for something more exciting? My best friends in the world are off having amazing adventures. They might not admit it, because they don't want to make me feel bad (Gifty even pretended to be homesick to spare my feelings), but all three of them are going to come back changed. And I'll still be exactly the same.

I didn't know what was worse. That I'd spend the entire summer behind this counter, or becoming a tutor, arguably the nerdiest possible way to earn extra cash.

But Lucas thought I was good at it. And I don't think he was just saying it to be nice. I think he meant it.

"What have you got to lose, May?" I mumbled to myself.

"What was that love?" Said the old lady whose chicken chow mein I was meant to be ordering.

"Oh! I said, that'll be £7.50," I said, smiling brightly.

*

After I got home from my shift, showered (it's where I do my best thinking) and updated my journal for the day, I realised that Lucas had a point. There was no harm in tutoring because no one needed to know besides me. I didn't need to tell my friends and there's no reason anyone at school would find out. By the time I'd finished conditioning my hair, it seemed like a good idea. There'd be no need to buy ingredients and there was no way Jenny could accidentally ruin it with pink peppercorns.

But, I was going to need her help.

I walked into the living room where Jenny was watching YouTube videos on the TV. "I've thought of a way you can earn my forgiveness," I said. "If you do this for me, I'll stop giving you the silent treatment."

Jenny paused the TV and sat up straight. "What is it?"

I was taken aback by her curiosity. I expected her to roll her eyes and ignore me, but she seemed interested in my proposition. Maybe the silent treatment was getting to her?

"I need you to design some flyers for my next business. I'm going to be a private tutor. Lucas said his cousin makes loads of money from it."

Jenny wrinkled her nose but didn't say anything. "Erm, sounds . . . fun?"

"I don't need you to find it interesting! I just need your art skills to design the flyer."

Mum was cooking dinner in the kitchen and chatting to Andy (well, lecturing him about his "prospects") so we went upstairs to our room and got to work. I told Jenny what info I wanted on the flyers, and she designed the rest while I wrote postcards to my friends (I was a bit behind). Twenty minutes later, she'd drawn a seriously impressive design.

"Wow! Why aren't you this efficient with your homework?" I asked.

Jenny pulled a face. "Because homework is boring and this is fun, obviously!"

"I'd much rather do homework than draw. I'm so bad at it," I said.

"Good! It gives me a chance to be the best at some-thing for a change," Jenny mumbled.

"What do you mean? You're good at loads of things," I said.

I wasn't just saying that. I wished I had Jenny's confidence and creativity and don't-give-a-hell attitude.

"Not at school. Not like you and Andy, anyway. You guys are in the top sets for virtually every subject," she said.

"But look at your talent!" I said, pointing to the paintings and sketches she'd sellotaped to the bedroom wall. "I've got to draw a postcard for Sunita, and it'll be stickmen because I'm so rubbish."

"Like Mum and Dad care about me being good at art! You know they don't think it's a serious subject."

I sighed. I couldn't argue with her there.

"Maybe it doesn't matter what Mum and Dad, or anyone, thinks," I said.

But did I really believe that myself?

"Whatever," Jenny shrugged. "So, what are you gonna draw on Sunita's postcard?"

I laughed. "Like I said: stickmen! It was Gifty's idea, she's an artistic genius like you. I doubt Sunita will even have time to look at it properly. I bet she's having too much fun in France."

"You must really miss them," Jenny said.

I nodded. "Only two more weeks until they're back! It helps if I stay busy, hence the second job."

"Do you like the flyer?"

"I love it. Apart from the bit that says I can help with GCSE prep."

"What's wrong with that?"

"Jen! I haven't even started my GCSEs; how can I help someone out with theirs?"

"Because you've been reading thick books since you were ten. You could so help someone out with their GCSEs," Jen said. "Plus, you can charge more."

I couldn't argue with that logic.

"I'm going to photocopy it at the library and post them through doors. Maybe not at No. 19, though . . . Jenny, you should have seen her face!"

"I didn't need to see it. I heard her from the garden!"

We both laughed so hard that we didn't hear Mum call us for dinner. She knocked on the bedroom door and told us it was time to eat.

"Nice to see you girls getting along," she beamed, when she saw us together.

The next day I went to the library and photocopied

the flyer before my shift at the takeaway. I was doing the post-lunch shift, so it was absolutely dead, and there was no Lucas to keep me company. The stack of flyers sat on the counter by the till (obvious to customers, but out of sight from Dad in the kitchen), but I couldn't work up the courage to hand them out.

I thought about posting a few on the way to the takeaway, but every time I approached a front door cold dread seeped into my stomach, and I bottled it. I would have to ask Jenny to do it for me. Although, I wasn't sure how many favours she had left in her.

I passed the slow shift by writing in my journal, which I kept hidden by the till. If Mum or Dad popped their head out, I could stuff it under a stack of paper napkins. My friends don't get why I liked to write in my spare time (when I told Sunita about it, she pulled a face like she'd drunk sour milk). I explained it by saying it was like Gifty and her painting, Dawn and her singing and Sunita and her impressions of people falling over: it's just how I express myself. Between the pages of this journal, I can say what I want with no one to judge me or tell me that my dreams are a waste of time.

When my shift finally crawled to an end at five

o'clock and Lucas arrived for his shift, I'd given away a grand total of three flyers. And I'm pretty sure the people who accepted them thought they were napkins.

I held up the stack of flyers to show Lucas. "Don't say I told you so!"

Lucas broke into a dimpled grin. "I told you so! Nah, seriously, May. This is such a good thing for you. You're gonna get too big for this place and leave me, I know it."

"That depends on if people actually take the flyers. No one seems interested in a tutor," I said.

"Tunde gets most of his jobs through word-of-mouth. All you need is one good client and news will spread. Trust me. What subjects are you going to teach?"

"The most boring ones: Maths, English, Science. I do pretty well in those subjects," I said.

"Oh! Before you leave, I have something to ask you. Are you doing anything this Saturday night?"

My mouth went dry.

"Yes!" I said. I surprised myself with my own enthusiasm. "I mean, yes, I'm free. Because I'm not doing anything this Saturday night."

Lucas looked so pleased. How did I not notice how

cute his smile was before now?

"Sick! Can we swap shifts? It's just that I've got somewhere to be this Saturday night," he said.

And he knew I was a friendless loser, who'd have nothing better to do on the weekend.

I tried not to let my smile falter. "Sure."

"May, you're a lifesaver," he said. "I owe you."

How was it possible to experience such a roller-coaster of emotions in just two minutes?! I went from feeling surprised to joy to crushing disappointment.

He probably had a date with a girl who didn't wear a hairnet or get excited about homework.

Just because he's kind to you, doesn't mean he fancies you.

I felt my eyes fill with tears. I had to leave.

Me and my stupid big mouth. "I-I'd better get home," I said, rushing out of the front door.

"May, wait!" Lucas called after me, but I pretended not to hear him.

It wasn't until I got home and into the bathroom that I realised I was still wearing my hairnet. Perfect.

"Any customers?" Jenny asked brightly, when I came out of the shower. She was sat on the sofa with Andy, who was reading a dense history book.

"Not yet," I said. "I only gave away a handful of flyers."

"Flyers for what?" Andy asked, closing his book. It was so heavy that it slammed shut.

"Don't tell Mum and Dad, but I'm gonna make some extra money tutoring. I want to stay busy this summer," I said when Andy raised his eyebrows.

"You're certainly doing that! I admire the work ethic, but you know you're meant to rest over the holidays, right?"

I shrugged. I didn't say that I was working to distract myself from the loneliness more than anything else. So I had something to show for the holidays, like my best friends.

"Andy promised to watch the Marvel Universe movies with me in chronological order," Jenny said.

"I did no such thing! Just *The Avengers*," Andy protested.

"That's what you think," Jenny said. "You can join us, May, on one condition."

"What's that?" I asked.

"You have to microwave the popcorn," Jenny said.

"You drive a hard bargain. Deal!"

After I made the popcorn and tipped it into the big

mixing bowl, I sat between Jenny and Andy on the sofa. I couldn't remember the last time we did this. Although Andy asked loads of annoying questions about the Marvel cinematic universe (he doesn't even own a TV!) and Jenny ate the popcorn extra-loud on purpose, it was kind of fun. For the first time that summer, I forgot that I missed my friends quite so much.

Dear Sunita,

I'm sorry to say this will be an embarrassingly short update. I can't believe that you've been in a plane and flown to a completely new country. I haven't even left our town!

I've tried my hardest to stay busy over the summer. Jenny and Andy are here, I've taken on extra shifts at the takeaway, and I even have a small business idea.

The group chat is totally silent, which I have to admit, is making me sad. I could really use your advice about matters of the heart. I know you'd be able to cheer me up in seconds ... but a postcard could take days! How did long-distance relationships cope before the internet?! No wonder everyone in the olden days popped their clogs in their fifties. They were probably bored to death.

Yours Forever, M x

P.S. I can't draw so I let Jenny illustrate this postcard seeing as she's such a good artist. She claims it's an abstract piece entitled 'My Side of the Bedroom'. I suspect she's inspired by real life events ... but who can say?

CHAPTER TWELVE

GIFTY

Every day I went to the village square, sat on the bench, and giggled with the girls. And every day I pretended not to look at the mural being painted by the mysterious girl in the paint-splattered check shirt.

She started by coating the beige brick wall with a smooth, even coat of white paint, which stood out brilliantly against the grey-blue sky. Then she got on a ladder and sketched out a pattern with a smaller paintbrush. It was too faint for me to see from a distance, and I longed to know what she was creating.

Little did I know, I was about to get my chance. After a particularly vicious rainstorm that had me at home all day, the roof sprang a leak and water began to drip from the ceiling over dinner. You'd have thought the entire house was flooded; the fuss Granny made over it.

Grandpa got up and shuffled over to the kitchen door.

"Jonathan, don't you dare get on that ladder!" she yelled. "I won't have you climbing the walls after your injury."

Grandpa sighed and turned slowly to face Granny. "I am merely going to get a bucket."

I swear it was the most he's said in front of me for the last few weeks.

It rained and rained all night, lashing against the window panes in my bedroom. But rain storms were only fun when you had someone to share them with. If I were home, I'd be tucked up on the sofa between Mum and Dad, while we counted the seconds between the thunder and the lightning. Dad claims that the number of seconds is equal to the number of kilometres the lightning is from us – something to do with the speed of light being faster than the speed of sound – but I wasn't sure if he'd made that up.

In the morning, I was woken up by chatter outside

the cottage (the windows really were very thin). I recognised Granny's voice, but the others I didn't. I tried to get back to sleep but they were talking too loudly. At least the rain had stopped.

I threw the duvet cover off and crawled out of bed to peek out of the window. My silk scarf had slipped off in the night so my hair was a bit all over the place. I ducked to avoid being seen then peeked out the window.

Out of nowhere, a face appeared. I screamed and leapt back.

It was *her*. The girl who painted the murals.

What was she doing on a ladder outside my bedroom window?!

I recognised her paint splattered shirt and her brown ponytail. Her green eyes were wide with shock, which made two of us.

"Oh! Sorry!" she said before ducking back down.

Was this some weird hallucination? I heard some muttering and then Granny's voice. "Ah, my granddaughter is a late sleeper."

I put a dressing gown over my bed t-shirt (of course it had to be the unicorn one – very mature) and drew the curtains. I was well and truly awake now.

I got showered and dressed in the bathroom then came downstairs for breakfast. Even though I'd thoroughly embarrassed myself in front of Mural Girl, I was curious about her. I hoped she was still there.

"Ah, Gifty, you're finally awake!" Granny said as I wandered into the kitchen. She put down her tea towel. "I'll get your breakfast on."

"It's fine, Granny. I can make myself some toast," I said. "Who was that earlier? On the ladder?"

"Ahh, I hope the wee lass didn't give you a fright!" Granny chuckled. "Mr Wright and his daughter came to fix the leak in the roof. He's our local handyman. I know your gran'da prefers to fix things himself, but ever since the accident he's been on strict orders not to–"

"Wait, what accident?" I asked. I know it's rude to interrupt but that's the only way to get a word in edgeways with Granny.

Granny made a face. An 'I've-said-too-much' sort of face. "Never you mind, pet. I'll fix your toast. Why don't you ask Mr Wright and Ellie if they want a cuppa?"

"Sure," I said.

I could totally do that. So why was I feeling so nervous?

I walked around to the back of the house and found Ellie holding the ladder while her dad was at the top.

"Do you want a cuppa?" I asked.

"Where's the unicorn gone?" Ellie smiled.

I couldn't help but blush. "Those were just my pyjamas."

"Sorry, I shouldn't tease. I'd love a cuppa."

"Me too!" Mr Wright yelled from the top of the ladder.

When I got back to the kitchen, Granny had already assembled three cups of tea on a tray with a stack of biscuits. My toast (the thick white bread Mum would never let me eat at home) was being buttered and cut into neat triangles. How did she do that in such a short time? I thought I was gone for about thirty seconds.

"Ellie and Mr Wright never turn down one of my oat biscuits," Granny smiled. "You can set this tray on the garden table, then come back for your toast."

I did as instructed. But I didn't want to put the tray down and leave. This was my best chance to find out more about Ellie. It's not like I was going to talk to her when I was hanging out with Isla, Skye and Megan. They'd made it very clear what they thought of her.

While Mr Wright went to his van for more supplies, I was left alone with Ellie. It would have been rude of me to leave.

"So . . . I think I've seen you painting in the village square. What are you working on?" I asked.

Ellie dunked one of the sturdy oat biscuits into her mug of tea. "The corner shop owner commissioned me to do a piece," she said proudly. "Pretty much anything I want, really."

"No way! That's so cool," I blurted out.

Ellie looked surprised by my enthusiasm. "You like to paint?"

I shrugged. "Sometimes. I mean, I used to. Do you live around here all year round, then?"

"Yeah. Where else would I live?"

"It's just that some of the friends I've made only come here for the summer break," I said.

"Oh. Those girls," she said. "I'm here all year round, and during the summer I work with Dad for extra cash. The old man could use some help."

"Oi! I heard that," Mr Wright yelled from around the corner.

"But I know what you mean. Everyone in this village is getting on a bit, and there's not much here for young people. You London types must be bored stiff," Ellie said.

"Oh, I'm not from London. I'm from a small town in Kent called Northstone. But it's bigger than here. We do have a high street at least," I said. "And considerably less rain."

Ellie shrugged. "I don't mind the rain. My mum moved to Glasgow when my parents split up, but I actually prefer it here. Everyone knows who I am. It's just . . . easy."

"Gifty, your toast is stone cold!" Granny called from the kitchen.

"I'd better have my breakfast," I said. But I didn't make any effort to move.

"Feel free to help out with the mural, Gifty. I'm there most afternoons," Ellie said.

I nodded. "Sure. See you later."

I went back inside for breakfast and chewed my cold toast to a tasteless pulp. How was I going to avoid Ellie while I was with my new friends?

But more importantly . . . why didn't I want to?

*

I'd fallen into a routine. On the days where it was dry, I hung out with the girls in the village. Sometimes we walked to the big shop and bought iced coffees in cans (I could never get used to the bitter taste . . . plus caffeine gives me the jitters), but we mostly stayed in the same place. I timed my visits so that I went home just before lunchtime because a) Granny would have a meal ready for me and b) because I had noticed that Ellie turned up with her paints in the afternoon. Although I was curious about her, I didn't want our paths to cross in front of the girls. They didn't have anything nice to say about Ellie.

On the days where it was rainy, I had no choice but to stay in the cottage. Sometimes that was a relief. It meant I didn't have to bother with make-up or trek around in my new heeled boots. I could be myself.

But that didn't relieve the boredom.

I remembered that May's birthday was coming up on the nineteenth and that gave me an idea for a project. It wasn't like I could buy anything for her, because I'd spent my money on clothes. And there wasn't anything worth buying from the village anyway, unless I got her some dusty boiled sweets from the corner shop.

The bad memories from my last crafting experiment were beginning to fade. I could tell, because my hands itched for something to do. I helped Granny with her latest batch of biscuits, and I had the urge to sculpt the dough into something more interesting than a circle.

Yes, being artsy was a bit babyish. But I had no internet, no books and no one to talk to besides Granny (Grandpa was still being silent and mysterious). I spoke to Mum and Dad every few days on the landline, but our calls didn't last for long. The phone was in the living room and Grandpa spent pretty much all his time there watching TV. It felt like I was intruding in his space.

Besides, Granny went out of her way to get me art materials. It would be rude not to use them. Sure, the selection was a bit limited compared to what I was used to; I missed my bright-striped washi tape and glittery stickers. But I could still pull together a decent birthday card with what I had.

I cleared a space on the kitchen table while Granny

podded fresh green peas into a ceramic bowl. At first, I wondered why Granny was always cooking something when there were just two other people in the house – we really didn't eat that much. Then I realised we shared a common trait: we both needed something to do with our hands.

I unpacked the carrier bag full of goodies and she beamed. "I hope you find something useful there, pet."

"I'm going to make a birthday card for one of my best friends. She's the last of us to turn fourteen," I said.

I stared at the coloured paper and watercolour paints, waiting for inspiration to jump out. May liked books and baking and being on time. How could I turn that into an attractive birthday card?

It bothered me that an idea didn't just leap out. It was weird. I wasn't used to waiting for inspiration to strike. It was just always . . . there. But I hadn't done anything creative in weeks. Had I lost my creative muscle?

Granny hummed along to the classical music on the radio, while she methodically podded the peas in a swift movement. I don't know if she realised it, but she was doing it in time to the music. It was like a mesmerising ballet of the hands.

Without saying anything, I picked up my sketchbook and a grey pencil. Then I let the pencil flow, capturing her movements onto the page. I forgot all about the birthday card and focused on sketching Granny while she sat in front of me. When she got up to prepare the peas, I filled in the gaps with memory.

I spent the rest of the afternoon glued to the kitchen chair. I must have gotten up at some point to fill an old jam jar with water and use it to moisten the paintbrushes, but I don't remember. For the first time since arriving here, I finally felt like myself again.

I was so absorbed by my painting that I didn't stop until Granny asked me to lay the table for dinner.

I held the piece of paper, still wet with paint, by the corners and lay it on the end of the table to dry.

"Just two places tonight, love," Granny said. "Your gran'da will be taking his dinner in bed tonight. His hip's playing up."

"Something to do with the accident?" I asked.

Granny smiled weakly and nodded. "He had a nasty fall and hasn't quite been the same since. It's such a pity. Jonathan is a wonderful artist, you know. That's where you get it from." Then her eye caught my still-wet painting. She turned to look at it.

"Is that me? Podding peas?" Granny asked, bewildered. "Oh, you clever thing."

I suddenly felt shy. "It's just something small."

Granny looked up at me, her eyes filling with tears. "Oh, Gifty. I adore it. Your mother said you were talented, but I never expected this!"

I felt my cheeks go red. Although I loved nothing more than my art getting compliments, it still made me a little embarrassed to be the subject of praise.

"Why would Grandpa's hip stop him from painting?" I asked, eager to shift the attention away from my painting. And I was curious.

"Oh, he never painted. He was a carpenter. He practically built every stick of furniture in this house!" Granny said. "That was his creative outlet. I have cooking, you have painting, and he has carpentry. But he can't build much when he can't stand up for longer than a few minutes at a time without pain."

"But he was standing up when you both came to meet me at the train station," I said.

Granny tutted. "I did tell him to stay in the car, but he wouldn't have any of it. He was dying to see you, Gifty."

"Really?" I couldn't help but sound surprised.

I relived every interaction I'd had with Grandpa since arriving. Since learning about his accident, it painted everything in a new light. What I assumed was indifference or dislike was actually something else: sadness.

I couldn't imagine how I would cope if my favourite hobbies caused me physical pain. I had gone just a few weeks without painting, and I didn't feel like myself at all.

"Don't mistake his quietness for indifference. He's just had a tough time of it lately," Granny said. "Now, be a good girl and take this tray up for your gran'da."

I picked up the dinner tray and slowly, carefully made my way to the bedroom upstairs.

Dear Dawn,

If time in London is flying by, then time here must be going backwards. It is so unbelievably quiet but I'm kind of used to it now. I think I might be turning into what mum calls a country bumpkin: I heard an ambulance siren recently and jumped out of my skin. It was the first traffic noise I'd heard in weeks!

I'm so glad that your cousin is showing you the sights and sounds. I've never thought of you as a people pleaser, but what do I know?

Granny and Grandpa couldn't be more different. It seems like Granny's life goal is to get me to have seconds and thirds (she must think I have four stomachs like the cows in the field behind the garden) while Grandpa is . . . quiet. The curious part of me wants to figure out why.

The painting on the front of this postcard is of the view from my bedroom window. Please note the aforementioned cows (you're lucky I can't paint smells, that's all I will say).

Lots of love, G x

CHAPTER THIRTEEN

SUNITA

When the time came for Thibault to pick me up for our date, I'd already been wide awake since five o'clock in the morning. When he asked me if I like to 'ike, I had no idea what he meant. Maybe it was the French word for 'romantic picnic for two'? But it didn't matter. We were going to spend the morning together, just us.

I didn't know what time he was coming, so I was showered and dressed by seven thirty, just to be on the safe side. I was happy with my outfit: my cutest sun dress and sandals, plus a leather crossbody bag that was too small for me to wear for school. Then I guzzled breakfast (three rounds of Nutella on toast – last night I was so annoyed with Anand that I barely ate anything) and sat on the little bench outside the chateau. As soon as I saw him, I planned to get up and meet him down the road so we could leave without my family interfering.

It was nearly eight thirty before I saw him come down the road. I almost didn't recognise him: his usual cool but classy outfits were replaced with cargo shorts, a plain t-shirt, a sun hat, and a giant rucksack. And yet he still managed to make it work.

"*Bonjour*, Sunita!" He waved and yelled.

I waved back, half-wishing he would keep the noise down. I didn't want my family to–

"Oh, Sunita. There you are!" Bryan said, poking his head out of the downstairs window.

Ughhhhh.

"We missed you at breakfast," he said. "What are your plans today?"

"I'm going out with Thibault. Just us two," I said pointedly.

"Yes!" Thibault said enthusiastically. "We are going on an 'ike."

"Hiking? Terrific" Bryan said. Why was he so cheerful about everything? It wasn't natural.

Oh. Wait.

Hiking?

That wasn't quite the romantic day I imagined. But, it was better than nothing.

"As luck should have it, we are preparing for a hike of our own today," Bryan said.

Oh *no*.

"Do you know the *Gorges du Verdon*, perchance?" Bryan asked.

Thibault nodded. "Ah, *oui*! I have been 'iking there every summer since I was a child."

Bryan clapped his hands together like it was the best news he'd heard all day. "Fabulous! We could do with a guide. I'm not the best at reading maps, you see. What do you say?"

"No! Sorry. We're busy," I said.

He was not going to take this moment away from me. He'd already taken away my mum. What more could he possibly want?!

"Actually, Sunita, this might be a good idea. *Gorges du Verdon* is a much nicer 'ike than the one I had planned but we can't get there on foot."

"Plenty of space in our rental car," Bryan said, with a bright smile.

It didn't look like I had much choice in the matter.

A Femme Fatale would be gracious and nonchalant. *Channel the FF, Sunita.*

"Fine!" I said through gritted teeth. "Sounds like a good idea."

We went inside and waited for everyone to get ready. Mum and Jack were staying at the chateau (Mum didn't do nature and Jack wanted to work on his breaststroke in the pool), so Bryan, Olivia and Anand were joining us on the hike. My favourite people.

"You're wearing . . . that?" Olivia asked as we stepped into the car.

I looked at her ugly khaki trousers and baggy vest. She was obviously jealous of my cute strappy sundress and sandals.

"Yeah, and?" I asked.

Olivia shrugged. "No reason."

I scooted into the back seat next to Thibault.

"Oh no you don't!" Anand said. "You need to sit in the front seat. Remember what happened the last time we went on a long drive?"

"That was years ago!" I protested.

"Sunita gets a little car sick," he said. "Especially after too much chocolate milkshake. Ever since then, she

185

always sits in the front seat. Otherwise . . ."

Then Anand made a fake-vomiting noise that was nauseatingly realistic.

I wanted to murder him.

"Fine! I'll get in the front seat," I said, just to get him to shut up.

We drove for about forty minutes to the hiking spot. I couldn't even talk to Thibault, because he was in the very back seat with Olivia. I tried turning around to get involved with the conversation but that made me feel queasy. I hated to admit it, but Anand had a point: winding country roads plus several rounds of chocolate spread on toast for breakfast wasn't a good combination. I stuck to looking out of the window and tolerated Bryan humming along to the French pop music on the radio.

I could hear Olivia and Thibault laughing and chatting. Clearly, my plan to become a Femme Fatale wasn't working at all. Maybe I just didn't have it in me to be the quiet and mysterious type?

Plus, it was *so* boring! I'd spent so much of this holiday trying to be something I wasn't, and it made me nothing but miserable. I may not be sophisticated like Olivia, a brain box like Anand, or freakishly sporty like Jack (I caught him jogging on the spot while waiting for someone to come out of the bathroom). And I may come up with silly fancy dress ideas that only my friends understood. But, as long as *they* got me, I didn't need anyone else to. Not even boys with sexy accents and smoky eyelashes.

I'd had it. I was done with being boring and grown-up. However I acted, it annoyed Anand regardless. And Thibault seemed way more interested in laughing at Olivia's French jokes than talking to me. So, I may as well have some fun.

"Sorry, Bryan. This music is awful," I said.

I turned the dial on the radio until I heard something vaguely familiar: an old Harry Styles tune! I blasted the volume as high as possible and sang at full volume to 'Watermelon Sugar'.

And it felt good. Like I was back home with the girls forcing them (nicely) to do karaoke with me in my room.

Anand rolled his eyes. But to my surprise, Olivia and Thibault joined in just as enthusiastically. I didn't expect Thibault to know the words, but he sang along to the entire song (the boy has taste, clearly). Bryan smiled and nodded, joining in for the chorus. Even Anand ended up singing a bit towards the end, which was the biggest shock. (He'd never had anything nice to say about One Direction when I was younger.)

By the time we finished our karaoke sing-along (nothing makes time go faster than singing your heart out), we had reached our destination.

"Woah," I said. "It's like an actual forest!"

When Bryan mentioned hiking, I thought he meant a big park. Like the one we have in Northstone, with an ice cream van and a small playground and a big patch of grass. But this was the proper outdoors. Everyone else around us had rucksacks and big old boots. I felt so out of place in my sundress and sandals.

A sloping dirt road led out from the car park, leading down to a shimmering blue lake. People swam and dived from the rocks. Thibault and Olivia marched up to the top of the rocks and took photos on his phone. It really was beautiful.

He didn't even wait for you.

Suddenly it all felt painfully obvious. The joking and laughing. The two of them sitting in the back seat. The compliments about her stupid little cakes.

Thibault was into Olivia, not me. That's why he was

hanging around. He didn't care how sophisticated I was, what I wore, or what I said.

I felt so unbelievably silly. I'd made another humiliating mistake yet again. Why did I think that someone who looked like that would even notice me?

"Oh, Sunita! I thought you had hiking shoes in the car," Bryan said, interrupting my downward spiral.

Anand burst out laughing. "Your feet are gonna be screamin'," he said.

"Sunita, I really don't think it's a good idea you hike in those shoes," Bryan said. "You might twist your ankle."

I shrugged. "Fine. I'll sit by the lake while you lot go on your nature walk," I said. "Wave to the mosquitoes for me."

I didn't care if I missed out on spending time with Thibault. Who walks for fun, anyway?! After that long drive, I just wanted to take off my sandals and cool my feet in the lake. My phone might not have any internet, but I did have my earphones and a three-hour playlist of my favourite summer songs.

Bryan looked conflicted. He obviously wanted to go on the hike, but he knew that Mum wouldn't like it if he abandoned me. "Are you sure, Sunita? I'll stay with you . . ."

Anand shrugged. "She'll be fine. Don't get lost or anything, alright? Mum will get upset."

Olivia sighed. "I did try to warn you about the shoes—"

"Yes! I know, Olivia," I snapped. "Sorry I can't be as perfect as you."

Then I stomped down the slope towards the edge of the lake and sat down. I had to make myself comfortable because I'd be there a long while. I had no towel, no swimsuit, no flip-flops . . . I hated to admit it, but Olivia had a point. They all did.

If I put in my earphones, lay down on the ground and closed my eyes, I could pretend it was a hot day at home and I was in the park with my friends. It was weirdly comforting. I let time pass by like that, letting song after song wash over me. After a while, I felt something hovering over me. I opened my eyes.

It was Thibault. He smiled down at me.

I pushed myself up and he sat down on the ground next to me. He handed me a bottle of water. "I thought you might need this."

"Thanks," I said. I can't lie, I was a little upset with him. This was meant to be our day out and he'd abandoned me for Olivia and the others. "Don't tell me you finished the hike already?"

"I let the others go on without me," he said. "I couldn't leave you behind."

I nearly spat out my water. "Really?"

He raised one eyebrow. "Of course. Is that a surprise?"

"Well, yeah," I said. "But you didn't have to come back here and check on me like I'm a little kid. You don't have to feel sorry for me."

Thibault looked confused. "Feel sorry for you? This is an English phrase that is new to me. Explain?"

I sighed. He wasn't into me, so what else did I have left to lose?

"I get that I'm not as smart or sophisticated as Olivia. It's okay if you like her more," I said. "You have nothing to feel bad about."

"I like Olivia very much. I also like you very much. I am friends with you both," Thibault said.

"No, Thibault. You *like* her like her. You . . . what's the word in French? You *j'adore* her. Right?!"

That's when the penny (or should I say *cent*) dropped. "You think I love Liv?! That is absurd," he said.

"Woah. Bit harsh, Thibault. I know she's dead posh and does that weird flicky thing with her hair every ten seconds, but–"

"*Non!* I mean, Liv is great. But I don't love her. How could I when I'm gay?"

"You are?" I asked.

Thibault chuckled. "You did not realise? Perhaps I need to wear my rainbow flag t-shirt more often."

"So . . . you're not into Olivia or me?"

Thibault shook his head.

"Then why do you like spending time with me? You laugh at my jokes and listen to what I have to say? Where I'm from, boys never do that unless they fancy you."

"Then they are idiots. You are so much fun! I think your family is really . . . how you say? Cool. I love spending time with my grandparents, but I am there to take care of them. I love them but it's hard work," he said.

Suddenly, I felt a bit ashamed. I hadn't asked Thibault any questions about his family at all. I liked looking at him and I liked the idea of him. But did I actually *know* him?

Not really.

I'd totally objectified him! I was a terrible sexist.

"Tell me about that," I said.

And he did. He told me that he had spent every summer holiday in the village ever since he was a child. For the first time, his older sister wasn't with him because she was starting a family, meaning that he had to look after his ageing grandparents. And he was a little lonely.

"That's why I was so happy to have met you, Sunita," he said. "I finally had someone my own age to talk to! And your family were so nice and welcoming."

I smiled. "You mean nosey busybodies?"

"That is another English phrase I do not know," he said.

"It means they need to mind their business. Listen, I'm glad that spending time with us has cheered you up."

"It has! I knew I liked you from the moment I saw your chicken impression at the butcher's," he said.

I sighed. I didn't blame him. "It was my finest work."

Thibault stood up. "We're wasting this beautiful nature. Come on," he said, offering me his arm.

I smiled and stood up. We walked arm-in-arm towards the shimmering lake.

Dear Gifty,

I can't believe it's been several weeks since we all spoke! You guys could have shaved your heads and gotten tongue piercings, and I would never know (just kidding - I would obviously know because I would get phantom pains and my tongue would tingle in solidarity). My point is, it's been a weird summer made even weirder without having my besties.

The cute boy and I are just friends, which makes it sound like something went wrong* but nothing did. "Just friends" is the best possible outcome, I reckon. I'd rather have a new friendship where I can be myself than twist myself into something new for a boy (or anyone).

I hope your granny's rice has improved? I can't wait to come back home but I must say I will miss the food. Mum is in holiday mode and doesn't care that I've incorporated Nutella into every meal since I've arrived. As soon as we get back to Kent, it'll be back to green veg and despair.

Missing u, S x

* I mean, it kind of did. But I have to explain the whole thing in person.

CHAPTER FOURTEEN

DAWN

It's official. I'm a terrible friend. It's been nearly one month since I saw Sunita, May, and Gifty. And . . . I don't think I miss them anymore? Or maybe it's that I've just gotten used to missing them, so their absence feels normal.

Whatever it is, I feel like I've betrayed them. In fact, there isn't much I miss about home.

I try to tell myself that Mum would be pleased with that. That she sent me here to enjoy myself, and that pining over home every day is a waste of her money and my time.

But I still feel guilty. Because I found myself researching drama schools in London. Not just summer schools, but real drama schools. If I really cared about my mum and my best friends, I wouldn't be able to even think about leaving them.

Like I said. I'm a terrible friend.

I never expected to love it so much here. Not just the lessons, but everything about my life here. I love taking the bus from Auntie Pat's flat to school every day. I love hanging out with Dante and Haniyah between classes and I love that Kiana actually talks to me now.

Mastering the city feels like unlocking a new level to a video game. The tube map feels familiar now and not like some complex, colourful web of lines on a board. It feels like it's mine. How can I go back to my little life after enjoying this type of independence for the entire summer? I feel like it's changed me, and the old Dawn will never return.

Take last night, for example. As a special treat, Fletcher organised for the entire class to see a surprise musical. He said it was strictly research and for educational purposes only, but I saw the slightest hint of a smile across his face when we all cheered. Maybe he wasn't such a dragon after all.

After lessons finished, we rushed home to get changed and met up again at the academy. I followed

Mum's advice and wore the nice black dress she packed for me (I'm usually a trainers-and-jeans sort of girl but, on the phone, Mum insisted I wear a dress for the theatre), but my outfit was conservative compared to my friends'. Haniyah wore an elegant chocolate brown gown that matched her hijab and Dante wore a sparkling sheer mesh vest with leather leggings and sky-high platforms. Whereas I thought I was pushing the boat out with a slick of lip-gloss and mascara, both my friends had the sort of make-up that belonged on a catwalk.

"Wow! You guys look incredible. Are we going to the theatre or London Fashion Week?" I said when I met them outside the tube station.

"Well, life is a fashion show and London is my runway," Dante said. They air-kissed me so they didn't smudge their foundation.

"Thanks babe," Haniyah said, leaning in for a hug. "You look cute too."

"I feel so underdressed compared to you guys." I said as we made our way to the theatre. I followed them because I had no clue where we were going. "Mum says I'm too young for foundation."

"And she's right!" Haniyah said. "Besides, you have

beautiful skin."

"Yeah. You're not a haggard witch like us," Dante laughed.

"You're only one year older than me!" I exclaimed.

"Really? I forget that," Dante. "You seem much more innocent than I was at your age."

"I blame my mum. She's super overprotective," I said.

"Then it would've been hard for her to let you come to London for the summer," Haniyah said. "She must really want the best for you."

I smiled. I never thought of it like that. I made a mental note to reply quicker to Mum's texts (she'd managed to get them down to once per day, down from five times per day – this was progress).

We walked through London's West End, past bustling restaurants and traffic-lined streets. The walk took much longer because of Dante's heels, which were killer on the cobbled roads. But we finally turned a corner and that's when we saw it.

"The Lyceum Theatre!" Dante pointed.

I turned and saw it: a giant sign flashing yellow and black.

"It's *The Lion King*!" I yelled. "Are we really going to

see *The Lion King*?"

Haniyah smirked. "I didn't think you were a Disney fan, Dawn."

"I'm not! That's for little kids," I said, remembering myself. "But this is my all-time favourite musical. It's the show that made me want to be on stage."

"You're *never* too old for Disney, Han," Dante said.

We found Fletcher and the rest of our Musicals class at the meeting point outside the theatre. He handed out our tickets and we walked the red velvet carpeted stairs up to our seats.

Even though I had seen this musical before at this very theatre, going with Mum when I was nine was a totally different experience. It was my first theatre trip, and I had no idea what to expect. I think I was more excited about the thought of interval ice cream than the show itself.

But this time I knew what to expect. I knew the soundtrack back-to-front and upside-down, I had listened to it so much over the years. And even better, this time I was watching the show with people who loved musicals just as much as I did.

"Woah, nosebleed seats!" Haniyah giggled as she collapsed into a chair. "I feel like I have vertigo."

We were as far from the stage as one could possibly be, but that didn't dampen my excitement. As long as I could hear the songs, I'd be happy.

"Beggars can't be choosers, honey," Dante said. "A free night out is a free night out."

I sat between Haniyah and Dante. The lights dimmed and a hush fell over the audience. The show was about to begin.

But while I was watching it, something unusual happened. I didn't just listen to the songs and mouth the words quietly to myself like I usually do. I actually pictured myself on the stage, amongst the singers and the dancers. I imagined what it would be like to wear the feathered headdress and the intricate make-up. I imagined myself climbing onto the stage and slotting into the show seamlessly. It felt like home.

Even though the show ended, and I'd clapped until my hands were sore, I didn't want the night to end. It was past ten o'clock (on a weekday!) but Auntie Pat didn't mind that I was staying out a little longer with Haniyah and Dante – just as long as I got a taxi home. Haniyah and Dante lived fairly close to me so we could all share a ride.

The street outside the theatre seemed busier than ever, despite the late hour. Men driving rickshaws covered in bright lights looked for customers outside the theatre, while coffee shops and ice cream parlours shone invitingly.

"I never expected everything to be so busy this late!" I said excitedly as we filed out of the theatre.

"Does your town shut at nightfall or something?" Haniyah asked.

"Nah, a few little shops and takeaways stay open late. But it's not like this," I said.

"So, what now?" Dante asked. "I can't do any long walks in these shoes, so please suggest something in a two hundred metre radius."

"How about some fro-yo?" Haniyah suggested. "I know a place around the corner."

I didn't know what fro-yo was (a hot drink? A snack? Who knew!) but I was eager to keep the magic of the night going. I don't know whether it was the magic of the show or the unusually warm late-night air, but the very last thing I wanted was to go home. I wanted to crystallise this night in amber and remember it forever.

Haniyah led us to a brightly lit cafe with a neon pink sign. Judging by the posters lining the walls,

I realised where we were going.

"Ooh, I love ice cream!" I said.

"It's not ice cream, it's fro-yo, y'know? Frozen yoghurt?" Dante said.

Yet another thing we didn't have back home. I was sceptical about the thought of frozen yoghurt, but didn't want to kick up a fuss.

We joined the queue, which was swelling with other theatregoers, but it soon moved quickly. I ordered a small plain fro-yo, which looked boring until I saw all the toppings that you could choose. Once again, London won on the snack front.

We sat down on padded pink seats and huddled around a small table.

"So . . . what was your favourite bit?" I asked.

"The opening, obvs!" Dante said. "When the costumed singers popped up in the aisles? I was gagging!"

"Everyone loves that bit," I said. "But my fave is when they sing *Can You Feel the Love Tonight*. It's so romantic! I listen to the soundtrack all the time. In fact, I fall asleep listening to it."

"Wow!" Haniyah said. "You really like musicals, huh?"

I looked at them both. "Don't you?!"

"I thought I did, until I met you!" Haniyah said.

"Well, you're in the right place," Dante said. "If you want to be on the stage, you have to be in London."

I wouldn't be in London for much longer. I quietly ate another scoop of fro-yo (it wasn't chocolate ice cream, but I was starting to like it).

"Dante, don't say that! I'm sure Dawn can continue her musical career in Kent," Haniyah said.

Dante shrugged. "I am sorry, but no. London has a vibe, an energy, a certain . . . *je ne sais quoi*. It's the place to be for artists like us."

I didn't like the sound of this Kent slander. Only I could slag off my home town.

"Excuse me, but I've managed to be an artist just fine without London," I said.

"Suit yourself," Dante said. "You've come a long way since your first ever lesson with Fletcher. But talent like yours needs nurturing all year round, not just during the summer."

"It's funny you mention it," I said. "Because I was looking at drama school websites last week . . ."

"Seriously? You'd move to London?" Haniyah said.

The words were out there, and my feelings were

undeniable. *Move to London.*

I shrugged and looked down at the table. "It was just an idea. I couldn't leave Mum, anyway."

"Why not? I'm sure Mum has a life of her own!" Dante said.

I shook my head. "Actually, she doesn't. She sacrificed her own dreams for me. When Dad died, she gave up her singing career and became an accountant. An accountant! She does maths all day."

Dante blinked. "What's your point?"

The remains of my fro-yo puddled in a melted mess at the bottom of my cup. I wasn't hungry any more.

I sighed. "My point is that I can't just up and leave. Especially for something that she doesn't want me to do. I need to carry on Dad's legacy."

"And, has your mum actually told you this?" Haniyah asked.

"She didn't need to!" I snapped.

Oh *no*. I was rude to my only friends here and now they were going to hate me.

"Sorry, Dawn. I didn't mean to upset you," Haniyah said.

I felt my face go hot. "You didn't," I blurted out. "I didn't mean to snap. I'd better get going," I said.

"Oh no you don't!" Dante said as I rose. "You're getting a taxi home with us. If you run away and don't make it home, it'll be a stain on my conscience."

"I can tell it's a touchy subject," Haniyah said. "I won't bring it up again, promise."

I smiled, relieved that she wasn't upset with me for snapping at her. But I was still embarrassed. They must think I'm so childish and sensitive. Maybe I'm not as grown-up as I thought.

*

A few days later, I was doing the washing up after dinner. It was funny how Kiana always had somewhere to be when I was doing chores . . . but I didn't mind. While I washed up, Auntie Pat portioned the dinner leftovers into plastic tubs and kept me company. Sometimes she played Dad's music and told me stories about their wild nights out in the nineties that involved "one too many lemonades".

I was always eager to hear any story about Dad from Mum, even the ones I'd heard one thousand times or more. The stories were as familiar as my old teddy bear with the missing eye, or the old living room armchair that is perfectly moulded to my body (Mum thinks it's an eyesore, but I refuse to part with it). It was impossible for me to get bored of them.

So, when Auntie Pat had new stories for me about Dad's childhood and teenage years, I was all ears. It was partly why I volunteered to do the washing up after dinner.

"Your dad wasn't always this good at playing the guitar," Auntie Pat said. She was hilariously honest. "Forgive me for speaking ill of the dead but he used to be terrible. Terrible!"

I laughed. "Mum never told me that."

"This was long before your mother met him. Before Lloyd was a big big singer, he was a bird-chested ten year old boy who couldn't play in tune," Auntie Pat chuckled.

"Oh, my word, your dad just adored you," she continued once the song had finished. "He called you Miss Cutie because he said you were the cutest thing he'd ever seen. I wish he could see you now."

"Mum said he'd be really proud of me. With the singing and stuff," I said quietly.

Auntie Pat shrugged. "He'd be happy to see you *happy*. That's all most parents want, sweetness."

We were interrupted by my phone ringing. It was

Mum video-calling me.

"I'd better take this, Auntie Pat," I said and dried my hands.

"Hi Mum!" I waved to the camera. She was coming out of the office and walking to the car park.

"It's good to see your face, sweetheart!"

"Another late night at work?" I asked.

"May as well. The house is so quiet without you. Are you having fun? How are rehearsals for the Extras? I've booked my train for next weekend!"

"It's all going well. Our teacher got us free tickets to *The Lion King*! It was epic," I said.

Mum opened the car door and slid into the driver's seat. "That's nice, I guess. I would have thought a real gig would make more sense though," she said.

Of course. Mum doesn't know I'm doing the Musicals class.

"Well, they can't exactly take a bunch of fourteen-year-olds to a concert," I lied quickly. "Something about health and safety."

Mum nodded. "Of course. Not to worry, petal. I'll take you to a real concert when I'm in London."

I smiled weakly. "Can't wait."

"But the highlight of my trip will be seeing my

babygirl on stage for the first time. Have you decided which one of your dad's songs you'll be singing?"

Mum thought I was performing one of Dad's songs?

My stomach plunged. If it showed on my face, Mum didn't notice. She was too happy.

"In fact, don't tell me! I want it to be a surprise," she continued.

I managed to plaster a stiff grin onto my face. "Err, okay. It'll be a surprise," I muttered.

"Okay my darling. I'd better get home. A hot bath is calling my name. I miss you loads but one thing I don't miss is you hogging the bathroom," she chuckled. "See you next week."

I ended the call and felt like bursting into tears. Mum was coming to the Extras and expecting me to perform one of Dad's old songs. She'll be gutted if I don't.

What was I going to do?

Dear May,

I hope all is well in sunny Northstone? I sent the group chat a message about the Extras next weekend. I didn't forget that it was on your birthday. Please don't feel like you have to ditch your birthday plans to see my show. In fact, I forbid you to do it! August 19th is your day and we will celebrate when I'm back. I already have your gift wrapped and waiting.

To be honest, I could do with some of your sensible advice. But giving you a phonemail feels like breaking the rules somehow. Like I'll have failed the challenge of our summer holiday. So instead of asking for help, I will put myself in your shoes and ask WWMD*?

Big hugs, D x

*What Would May Do. But you already figured that out.

CHAPTER FIFTEEN

MAY

Exactly five days after I printed my first flyer, it finally happened. I had my first client! It was a parent looking for additional English support (my favourite subject) for their teenager. And they'd signed up for six sessions upfront! I was so excited that the whole family heard my startled gasp of joy, and they demanded to know what was going on. Everyone was really happy for me, especially Dad who said that tutoring would look good on my university applications.

I prepped my notes, organised my pens and selected my finest notebook. I was given their address and I walked over on Sunday afternoon with Andy (he insisted).

The client lived in the same neighbourhood as Holly.

Even though I had tried to block out that entire experience, the waves of embarrassment flooded back. It turns out you *can* get PTSD from a fancy dress party. Who knew?

Andy assumed that my quietness was down to nerves. "Don't worry, May. You're going to be great," he said.

He walked me to the house, and we pressed the doorbell. An older man wearing a smart shirt answered the door with a cheery grin.

"You must be the tutor," he said. "I'm Colin. We're very excited to have you."

He invited me and Andy inside. "My son is in the dining room. Now, I should warn you that English is not his strong point," he added in a hushed tone. "But if he's going to get into my alma mater, he needs to have a solid English GCSE."

"Well, I aim to please!" I said in a fake cheery tone.

"Right, well. As I said, he's in the dining room," Colin said.

I left Andy to chat with Colin in the hallway. When he was satisfied that this wasn't a kidnapping plot in disguise, I heard him leave the house.

I followed the winding hallway down to the dining room ("It's the fourth door on the right!"). Because

I wasn't paying attention to the framed photos in the hallway, or the surname on the stack of letters on the table, I didn't realise who my client was until I opened the dining room door and . . .

It was *him*.

Scott Mallory looked up from the dining room table. "You must be the tutor."

This must be some sort of cosmic joke.

I nodded, unsure if he recognised me. "I'm May."

"*Golden Lotus*, right?"

So, he did recognise me.

I could leave. I could spin on my heels, make an excuse to Colin, and never darken their door again. I could block his number and duck whenever he came back to the takeaway.

No.

I wasn't ashamed of who I was. I wasn't ashamed of my part-time job or my family's business. I was actually excited to start my first ever tutoring session. Like Luke said, I'm really good at it. So why would I let someone like Scott Mallory force me into scuttling away?

I straightened my shoulders back. "Yes, I work in my family's business. And I'm also going to help you with this essay. Your dad said he wants you to get a headstart on GCSE English?" I asked.

Scott shrugged. "Waste of time if you ask me. I told Dad that, but he won't listen."

Great. My first student didn't even want to be here.

"I mean . . . GCSE English comes in handy in pretty much every career path," I said.

"Not in Premier League football," Scott said.

I raised one eyebrow, but didn't say anything. The boy was clearly delusional.

"Right, well. Your dad is paying me to help you plan this essay so that's what I will do. Do you have a copy of *The Catcher in the Rye*? What were your first impressions of the book?"

Scott shrugged. "It was a book, y'know?"

Wow. This was going to be harder than I thought. He didn't even have a pen!

I took a pen out of my pencil case and laid it in front of him.

"Okay . . . So let's start with—"

Then he sighed. "How about I save us both a lot of trouble?" Then he pulled his wallet out and laid several banknotes on the table. "Will fifty quid cover it?" he asked.

"I thought your dad was paying me? We agreed fifteen pounds an hour."

He smirked. Then it hit me. The money wasn't for the tutoring sessions.

"Let me get this straight. You're paying me to write your essay?" I asked slowly.

"The way I see it, it's a win-win. You get more money and I get Dad off my back," he said smugly. "And if you do a good job, there's plenty more where that came from."

He had a point. If I accepted the money, I wouldn't have to endure Scott's obnoxiousness during these tutoring sessions. I could knock out an essay with my eyes closed, especially if I was pretending to be Scott Mallory.

"There's no need to feel guilty, May. Fifty quid must be like five shifts at your little takeaway?"

That comment snapped me out of it. The ethics of faking essays for someone else aside, how could I consider working for Scott Mallory?

"Thanks, but no thanks," I said tartly. "Now, can we get on with the essay?"

I resolved to finish the session. After all, his dad had paid for it. But then I'd make my excuses and cancel the rest. I'd rather swim in a vat of grease than tutor Scott Mallory for much longer.

Suddenly the smug smile was wiped from his face. I guess Scott wasn't used to hearing 'no'.

"What's your problem? Stuck-up cow," he muttered.

I slammed my book shut. That was *enough*.

Scott crossed his arms and smirked. "Don't tell me *Teletubbies* girl can't take a joke . . ."

I stood up. "Want to hear a joke, Scott? How about that the boy too lazy to write a single sentence reckons he's gonna be a Premier League footballer?" I swept my notebook and pens into my tote bag. "You're rude and arrogant, and you might be popular now, but if you think anyone will care about you when you leave school then you are *sorely* mistaken. And . . . I want my pen back!"

I grabbed my pen and left Scott Mallory, who was stunned into silence, in the dining room. I bumped into Colin in the hallway.

"Tell Scott to keep his cash. I won't be doing his homework for him," I said.

Then I went home and didn't look back.

*

"I can't believe you really said that to Scott Mallory," Jenny said from the bottom bunk. I couldn't see her as I was in the top bunk, but I knew exactly the surprised look she'd have on her face.

Even though Jenny was in primary school, I'd brought her up to date with all the school gossip over the summer holidays, so she knew exactly who Scott Mallory was.

I loved that she was so impressed with this story. I'd already told it three times and each time I acted it out, my gestures became more dramatic. I couldn't wait to tell Gifty, Dawn and Sunita when they were back.

"On the downside, that's another side hustle ruined," I said. "There's no way I can work for them again. I'll be known as the tutor who stomped out in a huff."

"You didn't stomp out in a huff! You stood your ground," Jenny said.

"Thanks, Jen," I said. "But that doesn't solve the money issue. I had to refund Scott's dad for the tutoring sessions, plus I've spent my takeaway earnings establishing the brownie business."

"You can cash in my coins at the coin bank, if you want?"

I was touched by her kind yet naive offer. "That's sweet of you. But that won't cover a train ticket to London. Dawn's show is on the nineteenth and I really want to see her."

"But that's your birthday?"

"Yeah. It would be the best birthday gift ever," I said. "Anyway, it's getting late. Lights out, okay?"

"I like our night-time conversations," Jenny said softly.

"So, you're not desperate to get your bedroom back?" I asked.

There was silence, then Jenny's quiet snores. I wasn't going to get an answer now.

*

When my first shift with Lucas rolled around, I was nowhere near as nervous as I thought I would be. Even though the last time I saw him involved me a) thinking he was asking me out and b) running out of the takeaway with my hairnet still on, I was feeling pretty chill.

I guess telling a smug bully what you *really* think of them can have that effect.

But if Lucas thought that I'd embarrassed myself,

he didn't let on. He was his usual friendly self and I soon forgot that I had something to feel silly about.

"We missed your brownies on Saturday," Lucas said when he came back from his break.

"What do you mean?" I asked.

"My mum's hall party! Thanks again for taking the shift. It meant I could help Mum and my aunties set up the party and eat my weight in puff-puff," he smiled.

Saturday night was his Mum's party. Not a date! The relief was immense.

"Oh . . . it's nothing," I smiled. "Did you have fun?"

"As much fun as you can have while one thousand Nigerian aunties pinch your cheeks and tell you you're too skinny," he chuckled.

I burst out laughing. "I'll swap one of your aunties for one of mine. My mum's older sister always points out when I have 'too many' dumplings at family dinner."

"Why would she do that? You look amazing," Lucas said. Like it was nothing!

Was he this used to paying girls compliments all the time? I felt my face grow hot and he put on his apron all casually. Luckily it was my turn to go on break, so I had an excuse to leave and didn't have to explain my blushing fit.

I had a twenty-minute break so I walked to the little field opposite the takeaway and sat on the grass. It was a blazing hot day, but cool-ish under the shade of the tree.

I had to tell someone about what Lucas just said. Someone other than Jenny. I opened our group chat: the last message was dated July 29th. That was three weeks ago and, apart from Dawn's show invite, there were no other updates. Looking at the empty chat gave me a gnawing feeling in my gut.

These were my best friends in the world. So why was I feeling so nervous about breaking the silence?

Yes, they were off having amazing adventures while I was at home, alone. They were probably going to come back armed with stories and all sorts of new experiences, just like everyone else starting Year Ten. Everyone but me.

"Don't be a baby," I muttered to myself. "They're your friends."

I checked the profiles to see who was last online. Dawn was just an hour ago.

I bit the bullet and typed a message into my chat with her.

MAY: Dawn . . . I think Lucas likes me?

It was done now. I couldn't take it back. Immediately, my phone buzzed.

DAWN: Erm, what a bombshell?! Tell. Me. Everything.

I couldn't help it. I broke into a massive grin. I didn't care if it looked like I had nothing better to do, I typed out a massive answer as quick as my thumbs would go. I had a lot to tell her!

DAWN: May I've missed your essays!! Gifty and Sunita are gonna be so annoyed to miss out on this.
MAY: Crap. Is that the time? My break's nearly over. Catch up soon?
DAWN: Yes pls! I need to get back to rehearsals. Will I see you next Saturday? I know it's your bday so I understand if you can't make it. But let me down gently, yeah? X
MAY: Can I let you know in a few days? Depends what Mum and Dad have planned.

I already knew what Mum and Dad had planned. It was the same thing we do every year: my *yí mā* (Mum's older sister – the same one who monitors my dumpling intake) has a beautiful restaurant in Croydon where we celebrate everything from birthdays to graduations. It's one of my favourite places.

Auntie Vivian may be irritating, but she knows how to throw a party. Last year I invited Gifty, Sunita and Dawn, and they loved every minute of it. But they wouldn't be there this year.

The truth was, I wanted more than anything to see my friends at Dawn's show. But I'd wasted my pocket money on hare-brained business ideas that didn't go anywhere and couldn't afford the train fare (not to mention that I still owed Andrew money).

Plus, Mum and Dad would be so disappointed if I broke our tradition. We'd had birthdays at Auntie Vivian's restaurant since before I was born. I'd feel like I was abandoning my family, and that felt selfish.

I would see my friends at the end of August as planned. And that would be just fine.

Dear Gifty,

Sorry it's taken me so long to get back to you.
Coming up with postcard illustrations is hard
work!

You sounded a little sad in your last message.
I hope things have picked up since then? Trust
me, you have nothing to be homesick about.
Northstone will be here just as you left it.

I hope you've been more inspired to pick up your
paintbrush. The world needs your art, Gifty!

Are you going to Dawn's show on the nineteenth? I really want to go but the funds are
quite low right now (it's a series of long stories,
will explain later). Please tell me when I get to
see your face again!

Yours Forever,

M x

CHAPTER SIXTEEN

GIFTY

The next time I went to meet Isla, Megan and Skye, we didn't hang around in the village square. It started to tip it down and huddling under umbrellas was no fun. We shivered in the rain (did August pass Scotland by or what?) before Isla had an idea.

"Let's go to my house," she said. "We can hang out in my room for a couple of hours. Mum and Dad have gone shopping, so they won't bother us."

We all agreed it was a good idea. I mean, Megan and Skye agree with everything Isla does anyway. But I was genuinely pleased for the invite. The only house I'd seen since arriving here was Granny and Grandpa's cottage, and the change of scene seemed exciting.

Plus, I was kind of anxious about how I'd deal

with seeing Ellie. Ignoring her seemed plain rude but helping with the mural was a step too far if I wanted to stay friends with Isla and the girls. Going to Isla's house solved that dilemma instantly.

We trudged through village roads and muddy paths for about twenty minutes, until we reached a row of super modern-looking houses obscured by tall hedges. We walked up the paved driveway and Isla let us into the house using an electronic key.

"Shoes off, please. Mum will actually kill me if I get one speck of mud on her precious rug," Isla said.

We followed Isla up the stairs and through the corridors to her bedroom. It had a massive bed, huge TV, and floor-to-ceiling windows, but not much in the way of anything personal: books, photos, art. I guess if this is their holiday home, she's only here a few weeks per year.

I made a mental note to never allow Isla to come home with me. Granny and Grandpa's cottage looked like a home for hobbits in comparison to this mansion.

Megan and Skye made themselves comfortable on the giant beanbags dotting the floor, so I did the same. Isla lounged on her bed like a princess presiding over her subjects.

"Here's the Wi-Fi password," she said, handing around a small plastic card.

I was going to have Wi-Fi! Real internet for the first time in two weeks. When I pounced on the card, Isla burst out laughing.

"Oh em gee, Gifty! I forgot you haven't had decent Wi-Fi in ages," she said.

"Yeah. I bet your phone explodes with all the notifications," Megan said.

I smiled. I was excited to see what my friends had been up to over the last few weeks. As nice as it was to receive postcards from the three of them, it didn't make up for the constant chatting from morning 'til night.

My phone connected and it was flooded with notifications, vibrating loudly.

"See! I knew Gifty was popular," Isla said smugly.

But the notifications weren't messages from my friends. They were showing new followers on TikTok, marketing emails, and a bunch of text messages from Dad before he realised the best way to contact me was through Granny's landline.

Was there seriously *nothing* from my friends? That

couldn't be right.

I opened the group chat and double-checked. There was a message! A really long one from Dawn. Maybe she had some hot gossip from the academy? Her last postcard said that everything was hectic.

I read the opening of her message:

DAWN: Hey everyone! I'm inviting you to Bright Stars Academy's Showcase Extravaganza on August 19th! You can order tickets on . . .

My excitement fizzed away. Dawn had sent us a copy-and-pasted invite to her show in London. No exciting update or message to see how I'm doing. The last message before that was from before we left Northstone when we were all together. It felt like another lifetime.

It was a double whammy of disappointment. Not only was there no real news from my friends, but I also wouldn't be home in time for Dawn's show. They'd all be there without me! In London! While I was hundreds of miles away from my favourite people in the world. I wanted to cry it was so unfair.

"Babe, can I borrow your hair straighteners?" Skye

asked Isla. "The rain totally destroyed my hair and now it's gone all frizzy."

I wanted to laugh. Skye's hair looked bone straight to me.

Isla handed her the straighteners in their box. "Have you ever straightened your hair, Gifty?"

I shook my head. "Nah, Mum won't let me use heat on it."

I said it without thinking.

Isla screwed up her face. "What do you mean, she won't *let* you? Does she, like, control you or something?"

Megan and Skye giggled.

"I . . . I mean my hair doesn't react well to lots of heat," I stammered. "It damages the curl pattern."

Skye crossed her arms. "Oh yeah? How do you know if you've never tried it?"

"I think you would look soooo good with straight hair. Really glam and grown-up," Isla said.

"Me too!" Megan chipped in.

"And your mum's not here to get in the way," Isla said.

The three girls stared at me intently. Why did they care so much about what I did with my hair?

"Oh, it'll take ages. Like, literally hours. My hair is sooo thick," I laughed.

"We've got the time," Isla said, wielding the straighteners like a weapon.

She had a point. Maybe it would be fun to try a new style? Mum would never have to know.

But do you want to?

"Come on, Gifty! I want to be a hair stylist when I'm older and this would be a big help," Skye said. "I'm never gonna get the chance to style your type of hair. It's so . . . unusual."

And, before I could stop her, she leaned over and grabbed a fistful of my curls in her hands.

I flinched back.

"Chill out, Gifty," she said. "I was just–"

"Well, don't!" I snapped. "You are *not* touching my hair."

I surprised myself with how stern I sounded. Skye flushed pink and Megan looked down at the floor. Isla pursed her lips.

"Suit yourself," Isla said and handed the hair straighteners to Skye.

She played music through the TV, some Taylor Swift playlist, and the girls chatted like I wasn't there. But it wasn't like before when they were content for me to sit in the background. They were ignoring me on purpose.

I'd broken an unwritten rule. Because they'd allowed me to hang out with them, I was to do and say and act like they wanted. I had to admit, I was happy to go along with it – to a point. I don't know why, but the thought of them changing my hair was my limit. It felt like they wanted to change *me*.

What was I still doing there?

I pushed myself up and walked out of the bedroom silently. The girls didn't even look up. I tiptoed down the stairs in my socks, put on my wet boots and crept out of the front door.

Then I found myself with another dilemma. How was I going to get home? I had no clue where Isla's house was, but I could remember how to get to the village square. Then I'd be fine.

I walked down the slippery driveway and back in the direction I had come. I didn't remember it looking quite so wild a few hours ago. Were there really that many trees?

It was only four o'clock, but heavy clouds blocked out the sun, making it seem a lot darker. I ambled through the forest in a straight line. Or at least I thought I did, but twenty minutes had passed and there was still no sign of the village square.

That was when I started to panic. I thought about going back to Isla's and asking for directions. Maybe her mum and dad would be back from shopping, and they could give me a lift? But it was a silly idea. There was no way I could talk to those girls again.

And even if I wanted to, I couldn't head back. Because I wasn't entirely sure if the house was even behind me.

"Well done, Gifty," I muttered to myself. "You're well and truly lost."

I optimistically checked my phone and, of course, there was no data or reception. I tried to remember some of the outdoors skills we picked up while camping on a school trip. I could navigate using the path of the sun . . . but did it set in the east or the west? And I couldn't see the sun anyway!

Relying on my non-existent outdoors skills was hopeless too. Then I heard the roar of traffic. There were cars nearby! I followed the sound until I came to a clearing and saw a road through the forest. There were no signs or anything, but still. Civilisation was near!

I walked along the side of the road. It was getting close to seven o'clock now. Granny would be serving dinner and wondering where I was. I had never felt more alone. The odd car drove past, flashlights winking in the dusk, and I thought about sticking my arm out. I couldn't remember Granny and Grandad's address, but I could get a lift to the village and–

Oh gosh. A car was slowing down behind me. Why was it doing that?! I hadn't stuck out my hand or anything.

I sped up, walking faster and faster until I broke into a run.

Then the car *beeped* at me. I pretended not to hear it.

The car sped up and pulled up right next to me.

"Gifty! Is that you?"

I stopped. I knew that voice.

It was Grandpa.

I didn't know whether to feel elated or ashamed. I trudged back to the car and sure enough, Grandpa was sitting in the driver's seat.

"Get in, pet," he said quietly.

I obeyed and jumped into the front seat.

"It's not like you to be late," he said.

My eyes filled with tears. I felt so *stupid*. How could I get myself lost in this tiny village? If Mum and Dad found out, they'd never let me out of their sight again.

"Sorry," I mumbled. "Lost track of time."

Grandpa nodded. "Happens to the best of us."

*

The next morning, I felt nothing but relief.

Knowing I wasn't going to hang out with the girls every day was a weight off my shoulders. I didn't have to wear a new outfit or slap on make-up if I didn't feel like it. I would be lonely for my last week of the holidays, but at least I'd be myself.

That said, I did feel a little embarrassed about getting lost in the forest. Not just because it happened in the first place, but also because of how scared I'd felt. A part of me really did think I'd be wandering the forest until nightfall.

When I came in last night with Grandpa, Granny was very concerned. I don't think she bought my story about me losing track of time with my friends, but Grandpa said he'd picked me up from the village square. It was a small lie, but I appreciated it. And it meant that Mum wouldn't find out that I was wondering a forest while lost, at least.

Today my plan was to finish May's card. I was sad to be missing out on her birthday dinner with her family. I wonder if she's cancelling that so she can go to Dawn's show? I doubt it; May had the same birthday dinner every year. At least that made two of us who couldn't make Dawn's show. That made me feel a little less guilty.

After the breakfast table was cleared, I sat down and spent my time on May's card. I cut flower petals out of coloured paper and arranged them in an intricate blooming pattern across the card. I spent my time over it, agonising over the placement of every petal. As if the effort I poured into the card could make up for missing her birthday.

"That's beautiful, Gifty," Granny said. I was so absorbed by the card that I didn't notice her looking over my shoulder.

"Thanks," I said. "But I can't finish it now. I've run out of glue. Do you think they sell it in the village square?"

"No need to go all that way. Your gran'da has some in his shed. You'll have to search for it, though,"

Granny said. "The key's by the door."

Going to the shed seemed more appealing than going to the village square and bumping into the girls. But as I unlocked the shed door and pushed it open, it felt like I was intruding somehow.

I coughed. The piney smell of sawdust tickled the back of my throat. But once my eyes adjusted to the dark, I saw the craft room of my dreams. I couldn't believe that this treasure was hiding in here all this time!

A giant wooden table was stacked with boxes of oil paints and jars of paintbrushes. I saw blank canvases, sticks of unmoulded clay, and boxes of balsa wood. It was like someone emptied the contents of the school's Art department into one room.

An easel with a canvas laying on top of it caught my eye. I walked towards it. It was a still-life painting of a bowl of fruit. I recognised the blue patterned bowl from the kitchen table. But the painting was half-finished: only some of the grapes were painted a rich purple hue, and the blue of the bowl wasn't filled in. It was as though the painting was abandoned halfway through.

I remembered what Granny said about

Grandpa's accident. A dodgy hip shouldn't stop him from painting. If he can drive, he can sit on a chair and paint. So, what's the real reason he stopped?

I took my time looking for the glue. I eventually found a squeeze bottle of PVA glue in a giant drawer stuffed with craft equipment, but I found myself not wanting to leave. This shed had taught me more about Grandpa than the last three weeks combined. Suddenly, he didn't seem as much of an enigma.

I understood him a little bit more. I understood the pain of not being able to do what you love. And I wanted so badly to help him out of it.

Dear Sunita,

I'm pleased to know someone made friends! I had a fleeting friendship with some girls I met in the village, but then things got weird and I got lost in a forest. That thing you said about being yourself in a friendship is so true. My experience made me realise how lucky I am to have you guys (and how glad I am not to live near a forest).

Honestly, getting lost was the most thrilling thing to happen since I arrived in this place. Luckily Grandad came to the rescue!

It took several weeks but I think I finally understand why Grandad is so quiet. He's an artist, just like me, and I only found out a few days ago. It turns out we had loads in common all along! I have a plan to get him out of his shell. Even better, it involves a cute girl I met in the village . . .

I can't believe this is our last postcard! It's an extra-long one so I haven't done a drawing because I needed the extra writing space. Are you going to Dawn's show this weekend? I'm gonna miss it because my train home is on Monday.

Lots of love, G x

P.S. Granny's rice is still mush, bless her, but her biscuits and cakes are so good that I don't mind.

CHAPTER SEVENTEEN

SUNITA

Weirdly, ever since I found out that Thibault didn't fancy me, our relationship became better than ever. It was like it took the pressure off. And I could finally stop pretending! I decided that Femme Fatales should stay in 1960s French movies where they belonged.

Thibault had joined us for dinner most nights since the hiking trip. Tonight would be our last meal together, which was bittersweet. Don't get me wrong, I was super excited to see the girls again (not to mention sweet, sweet internet). But Thibault had wormed his way into my heart. Into all of our hearts! Even Anand was sad to see him go.

When we got back from hiking, we found Mum

and Jack sitting by the pool laughing. Even though I didn't exactly expect her to be deathly bored without us (well, me), it kind of hurt to see her look so happy with someone else's kid. I was so used to having Mum to myself, and this holiday we'd barely spent any time together.

You can sulk or you can do something about it, Sunita.

I'd spent so much of this holiday pretending, and not in a fun way like when me and the girls used to prank call our moany Geography teacher with fake names based on rock formations (no lie, this was one of the funnest nights of my life).

My inner voice had a point. Why couldn't I just be honest about wanting to spend more time with Mum?

So, the next morning, I woke up bright and early. I made a disgusting coffee (so glad I don't have to pretend to like this stuff anymore) and knocked on Mum's bedroom door.

She came out in a dressing gown looking all puzzled. "What's the matter, sweetheart?" she whispered.

I handed her a cup of coffee and she looked even more confused.

238

"Nothing's the matter!" I said. "I just wanted us to have a day together before we leave. Just us two. Here's your coffee. Meet me outside in thirty minutes."

"All right," she yawned. Mum wasn't much of a morning person even though she liked to pretend she was.

I met Mum outside the chateau with two bikes. "Come on, before it gets too hot. Let's get moving!"

Mum followed me on the bike, and we cycled down to the main part of the village. Seeing the restaurant and the butcher's reminded me that I had so many hilarious stories to tell the girls. That's the one good thing about humiliating yourself: let enough time pass and it'll turn into a pants-wettingly funny anecdote.

We left the village square behind and carried on cycling. A few minutes later, we arrived at our destination: the remains of a Medieval castle towered above us, crumbling and beautiful. It was taken over by trees but that only made it more magical. We stared up in awed silence.

"Wow!" Mum said. "How did you find out about this place?

"Thibault told me. I thought you'd like it."

I took off my rucksack (well, Anand's – I'd 'borrowed' it) and unpacked our supplies. A blanket to sit down on, a few squashed pastries, and a bottle of water ice-cold from the fridge.

I knew I wanted to have a romantic picnic for two while on holiday. I just didn't expect it to be with my mum. But whatever. A picnic is a picnic, right?

"I'm so glad we got to do this, thank you," Mum said.

"Me too," I said. "It feels like we've hardly spent any time together this summer."

"Honestly, Sunita, I feel like I've seen more of you this summer than any other school break," Mum said. "Usually, you spend all day everyday with your friends. I love that you have such wonderful pals, but I never see you!"

I never thought about it that way. "I guess I always expected you to be around."

"And I will be! Things with Bryan are going well, but I'm not going anywhere. What do you think of Olivia and Jack?"

"I mean, they're posh but they can't help that," I said.

Mum burst out laughing. It felt good to make her laugh.

"But it was sweet of Olivia to lend me her dress. And I'm sure Jack is nice, even if the only thing he can talk about is Rugby," I continued.

"He is rather obsessed, isn't he?" Mum said.

I tore a *pain au chocolat* in half and shared it with Mum. "Anyway, Anand seems to get on great with both of them. Jack actually made him laugh! I haven't seen him laugh in nearly a year."

Mum stopped eating and looked all sad. "It's been hard for him."

"Hard for him? What about *me*! He's always picking on me. And when he's not picking on me, he pretends I'm invisible. I feel like he wants me to disappear."

"I'll speak to Anand about that, okay? But go easy on him. Ever since–"

I couldn't believe what I was hearing. "I can't believe you're taking his side."

"Sunita, would you let me explain? It's been hard for him since the divorce. He took it way harder than you."

The best way to describe my dad is that he wears a suit and tie for fun. He is constantly grumpy and the only thing that will raise even the slightest hint of a smile is an excellent report. I guess Anand got on better with him because he's a smarty pants.

Maybe this sounds bad, but when Mum and Dad's divorce was made official, I didn't feel . . . anything. In fact, I was kind of relieved. Mum started to smile again. And we got her all to ourselves. What wasn't there to love?

"What do you mean, he took it harder?" I asked. "No offence to Dad, but him moving out didn't make a huge difference. He was barely there anyway."

"Well, I didn't help matters. When the divorce happened, I threw myself into work. You didn't really notice because you have your friends. But Anand did."

"You think having friends makes that much of a difference?"

Mum smiled. "You tell your friends everything, right?"

I nodded. "Pretty much."

"Anand struggles to open up in that way. Just like his father," she muttered.

"I don't see why he needs to take it out on me," I said.

"Oh, sweetheart. I didn't realise it was making you

so upset," Mum said. "Why didn't you talk to me about it sooner?"

"Because I thought you'd agree with him. Anand is always telling me how childish I am. Maybe it's true?"

"Have you ever considered that Anand is jealous of you, Sunita?"

"Jealous? Of *me*? I mean, I think I'm awesomer than him in virtually every way. But the teachers at school love him. The girls at school love him. And he thinks I'm a giant baby. Why would he be jealous of me?"

"Because you are completely and utterly yourself. It comes so naturally to you," Mum said. "I think Anand envies that."

I smirked. If Mum only knew the way I'd tried (and failed) to overhaul my entire personality this summer. For a boy!

I was quiet for a second. "So, you're telling me that my personality is my superpower?"

Mum laughed. "Pretty much, yeah. And as much as Anand would hate to admit it, I don't think he wants you to ever change."

"Well, that's something we can both agree on," I said. "Are you going to eat the rest of that *pain au chocolat*?"

*

We had until lunchtime before we had to leave for our flight, so I left my packing until the morning. Everyone else looked at me like I was mad when I told them over breakfast.

"I packed last night," Olivia said. "I can't stand the thought of being so last-minute."

"Live a little, Liv!" I said. "Besides, I can pack in ten minutes flat."

Okay, it took a lot longer than ten minutes. Especially because Thibault stopped by to say goodbye to us all. We exchanged numbers and I told him he had a place to stay should he ever be in Kent.

"Has anyone seen my rucksack?" Anand yelled down the hallway.

Oops. His rucksack was under my bed and covered in pastry crumbs.

I dusted it off and placed it outside my bedroom. "Oi, Anand! Your rucksack is here. Right outside my bedroom. For some reason."

Anand picked up the rucksack. "Funny, that," he said.

"Can I ask a favour? Can you help me carry my suitcase downstairs?" I asked.

"Yep. Where is it?"

"In my room. Can you also help me zip it up?"

Anand rolled his eyes. "You get five minutes!"

I sat on the stuffed suitcase while Anand tried to zip it up. "It's no use," he said. "You've just thrown everything in! You know you actually need to fold your clothes for them to fit?"

I didn't ask him to help me because I wanted a lecture on clothes folding. I wanted to see if what Mum said was true. Did the divorce really bother him?

Before I could stop myself, I blurted it out.

"Mum thinks you're jealous of me."

"Pardon?"

"I mean . . . she said the divorce hit you hard. Is that true?"

For a second, Anand looked like he was going to stomp out of my bedroom. But he didn't. He looked at me for ages and ages.

"I think it hit me harder than you," he said. "You never seemed that bothered."

"I guess I don't miss Dad as much as you do," I said. "I assumed you felt the same because you didn't say anything to me."

"How could I? You're Little Miss Sunshine. You

245

act like you've never had a negative feeling in your life," Anand said.

"You didn't seem to have any trouble talking to Jack," I said angrily. "In fact, you've talked more to him this summer than you have to me all year. And you don't even *like* rugby!"

Anand sighed. "Jack gets it, though."

I crossed my arms. "It's not my fault I like a laugh. It doesn't make me silly or babyish or–"

I had to stop mid-sentence because tears filled my eyes. I guess those names bothered me more than I thought.

"Look, I'm sorry. Okay?" Anand said. "My therapist says I need to stop resorting to anger when I'm feeling vulnerable."

I wiped my eyes. "You're seeing a therapist? I had no idea."

Anand nodded. "Mum thought it was best you didn't know. I was in a pretty bad way when Dad moved out. I basically didn't leave the house all last summer."

"I thought that's because you were really into your PlayStation?"

He laughed. "I can't lie, *Final Fantasy* got me through some dark times."

"*We're leaving in T-minus fifteen minutes,*" Bryan yelled from the hallway.

"How is that the time already?! Anand . . ."

"Don't worry, sis. I'm on it," he said, flipping open the suitcase. "But you have to learn how to fold your clothes."

Dear May,

Please don't hate me. I can't believe I didn't mail your postcard sooner. I did write it, I promise, but it's all out of date now. I wanted to start a fresh postcard filled with my latest musings, but all my best stories just have to be told in person. Not even a little illustration will do! So, frustrating as it may be, you will have to wait just a little longer for my news.

To make up for my lateness, I have a very lovely and very French birthday present for you. I will be back in Northstone the day before your bday – you will know because the scream of joy I will scream once I get the internet back will reach a two-hundred-mile radius. So, there's that to look forward to.

Missing u (but not for much longer!!)

S x

P.S. I am posting this at the airport, so I will arrive home before the postcard does. It would probably make more sense to give this to you in person . . . but where's the fun in that?

CHAPTER EIGHTEEN

MAY

"So, how did your tutoring session go?" Andy asked the second I walked through the front door.

It had been several days since my showdown with Scott Mallory, but I'd missed Andy because he had been working late.

I kicked off my trainers. "I won't be seeing him again. He really didn't want to be there, so trying to get him to write an essay was a waste of my time," I said.

Andy nodded. "I hear you. I tried to tutor as a side hustle at uni and I couldn't stand it. All those spoilt brats totally disinterested in learning."

I decided not to tell Andy that Scott wasn't only a spoilt brat, he was a bully. After all, he knew where he lived. I didn't need him to fight my battles for me.

"Right? And I wasted my entire summer trying to find a way to make money that didn't involve hairnets," I said. "My friends are back next week, and I have nothing to show for it!"

"If you're worried about paying me back, forget about it," Andy said. "Consider it an early birthday present."

I sighed. "It's not that. My friends are coming back from holiday with all of these new experiences. They've travelled, met new people, spent time away from home . . . and I haven't even left Northstone. The only thing I have to show for the summer is a slightly new way of styling my hair!"

Andy was visibly confused. I think the hair thing threw him. He can only style his one way, so it's not like he could relate.

"I don't think your mates care what you've been up to this summer," Andy said.

"They might not care but I do," I said. "I don't want them to leave me behind."

"They won't, you dummy!" Jenny yelled from behind the living room door.

"Jen? Have you been listening all along?" I asked.

She swung open the door. "That's not important. What's important is that you know that your friends are obsessed with you. I've barely spoken to my friends this summer because I sort of forget they exist when they leave school. Not you!"

I sniffed. "Yeah. We did all write each other postcards. I've heard from Dawn and Gifty, but not–"

"That reminds me," Jenny said. "This arrived while you were at work." She pulled a white piece of card from her dungarees pocket and handed it to me. "Tell her to use an envelope next time."

My heart leapt when I saw Sunita's tell-tale scribbles. She always writes like she's in a race. I read the postcard in seconds.

"She's back on Friday! So at least one of my friends will be there for my birthday dinner," I said.

Andy and Jenny exchanged glances. "Better tell Mum and Dad that we have an extra guest," Andy said.

*

The last shift before my birthday, the day before, was a solo shift. It was always slow on Friday afternoons but knowing that my birthday weekend was on the other side made it particularly excruciating.

251

Sunita wouldn't be back in London until late, so we agreed to see each other at my birthday dinner tomorrow. We'd take the train to Croydon with my family, so I couldn't exactly catch her up on my gossip (mainly about Lucas) with them all there. It would have to wait for another day.

Lucas arrived fifteen minutes before his shift began. There was something different about him. He seemed unusually quiet.

"All ready for Friday night?" I asked.

"Yeah. Ready as I'll ever be," he said.

After I got changed in the back room and waved goodbye, he stopped me just as I was walking out of the door.

"Um, May? This is for you. Happy birthday for tomorrow," he said, pressing a neatly wrapped gift into my hands.

"T-thanks," I stammered. It was my first ever gift from a boy! At least one that I wasn't related to.

I went to duck out of the shop, but he touched my arm gently.

The hint of a smile danced on his lips. "Don't open it until your actual birthday, okay?" he said.

I nodded. It was the safest thing for me to do

because I couldn't trust my tongue to form words.

I can't remember the walk home at all. But before I knew it, I was in the front door, running up to the bathroom (the only room in the house where I can get some privacy) and staring at the gift.

I was totally going to open the gift before my birthday. "Sorry, Lucas," I whispered.

The small parcel was wrapped neatly in shiny gold paper. I carefully loosened the tape and lifted it away from the paper so it came off in one clean sheet. I was going to treasure it forever.

I gasped. It was a journal. Thick, leather-bound with unlined cream pages. It was simple, but incredibly well-made. I could tell from how thick each page felt between my fingers.

There was no way Lucas brought this in North-stone. Our only stationery shop was a Rymans, and it didn't sell anything near this fancy (believe me, I knew their inventory inside and out).

I opened the first page of the journal. There was a note written by Lucas. It was the first time I'd seen his handwriting and I felt butterflies twirl in my stomach. Not because it was particularly nice hand-writing. In fact, it was a little messy. But because it was a part of him, I'd never seen before. It was the most intimate thing he'd ever done for me.

The inscription read:

Dear May,

I noticed your last journal was looking a little battered. Hopefully this one has a longer life.

Please use it wisely! Maybe start that novel? And if you do start a novel in the journal I bought you, you are legally obligated to name a character after me. I don't make the rules.

Happy birthday.

Lucas x

P.S. Give the money-making schemes a miss. If you become crazily successful and leave the takeaway, I don't know what I'll do.

One part of the inscription stuck out to me more than the rest, and it wasn't the kiss at the end.

Maybe start that novel.

Reading that line sent a tingle down to my toes. That's what I wanted to do! It might not be a side hustle that makes me money or gets me social media followers, but writing was the thing that made my heart sing. I'd been wasting my summer chasing things that weren't me at all, when I could have taken my journaling to the next level. I don't know how Lucas realised that before I did, but I was grateful.

I was reading the inscription for the thirtieth time when I was rudely interrupted by bangs on the bathroom door.

"Oi, May! You've been ages! What's going on in there?" Jenny yelled.

"Two minutes," I said.

I wrapped the journal back up in the paper and tucked it underneath my t-shirt. I'd tell Jenny and my friends about Lucas' gift tomorrow. For now, it was my little secret.

*

I was so silly to think that me and Sunita being apart would change anything. As soon as we saw each other on our phone screens, we picked up exactly where we left off.

Sunita was sad to be missing out on Dawn's show as well. Her mum was too busy to take her to London for the day, but I was secretly relieved. At least one of my friends would be there for my birthday. Dawn was totally understanding about us missing her big debut and assured us that her mum would be filming the entire thing.

Sunita and I had loads to tell each other about the past few weeks, and we could've talked all night if Mum hadn't called me down for dinner.

I was surprised to see the table laden with the red and gold tablecloth Mum reserved for special occasions, and the entire family sat around the table. Including Dad.

"Who's cooking at the takeaway if you're here, Dad?" I asked.

Dad waved his hand dismissively. "I asked a couple of friends. I didn't want to miss your mother's pork belly."

I sat down at the table. It wasn't like Dad to skip the Friday night shift. It was probably because Andy would be leaving soon. The summer was nearly over, and he was heading back to uni.

The evening started well enough. Mum's sticky pork belly was amazing, and it was kind of nice to have the entire family together. That is, until Dad made the mistake of asking how my tutoring was going.

"I'm not doing that anymore," I said. "It wasn't working out for me."

Jenny looked like she was about to say something, but stopped. I was relieved. The last thing I wanted to do was explain why I gave Scott Mallory a piece of my mind.

Dad's face was a picture of disappointment. "But, why? Tutoring would look great on your university application."

I dropped my chopsticks. *Here we go again.*

"It just . . . wasn't a good idea," I mumbled.

Dad sighed. "But it was! Students who have extra-curricular activities on their application are–"

Mum tapped Dad's forearm. "Not now," she said.

"Why not now? She will be applying for universities in just three years. Now is the perfect time for May to start setting herself apart from other Economic students."

There was silence for a few moments. Then I broke it.

"What if I don't want to study Economics?" I said.

Dad pretended like he didn't hear me and lifted a cup of fragrant broth to his mouth.

Mum smiled, ever the peace keeper. "We have plenty of time to decide. We don't need to make a decision now."

"Who's 'we'? You do realise this is my decision to make?" I said.

Dad carefully placed his broth on the table. "You can choose another course if you like. Such as Medicine or even Law."

I took a deep breath. "I'm going to study English Literature. Or maybe Creative Writing."

"You will do no such thing," Dad said calmly.

I wanted to scream. How could he make such a big decision for me and not even hear my side?

"That's not fair!" I yelled, the words escaping my mouth before I could stop myself. "You don't get to choose my life!"

The whole table froze. Even Jenny looked taken aback. I'd never shouted at Dad before. We had no idea how he'd react.

"Life isn't fair," Dad said quietly. "Believe it or not, your mother and I know what's best for you."

"You're not listening," I said, close to tears. "Can you at least listen to me?"

Dad gave an imperceptible shake of the head. "This

conversation is over."

I wanted him to shout back. I wanted him to scream and yell so I had something to fight against. But I couldn't argue with him like this. It was beyond frustrating.

The last thing I wanted to do was sit around a dinner table and pretend everything was okay when it wasn't. I was the only one of my friends who had a parent priming them for a life they didn't want. The thought made my head spin. I had to get out of the room.

I got up the leave the table.

"Where are you going?" Mum asked.

"Tell Aunty Vivian I won't be coming to the restaurant tomorrow. My birthday dinner is cancelled," I said through my tears.

I ran up the stairs and locked myself in the bathroom. I ran a scalding hot bath. By the time the bath tub was full, Mum had stopped knocking on the door to see if I was okay. I stayed in the bath until my toes were wrinkly and I couldn't cry any more, then slipped quietly into bed.

I checked my phone. It was nearly midnight and nearly my fourteenth birthday. I couldn't have felt more miserable.

*

When I woke up on Saturday morning, I remembered my argument with Dad before I remembered it was my birthday. The last thing I wanted to do was the long trek to Croydon with my family.

To be honest, all of them were in my bad books. Mum didn't stand up for me and my siblings stayed quiet too. I felt completely alone. It was a good thing I had my journal: writing down my thoughts helped me to make sense of the situation.

My thoughts were interrupted by a knock on the door. It was Andy.

"Happy birthday, sis!" he said cheerfully.

I grunted and rolled over.

"She only just woke up," Jenny said from the bottom bunk.

"It's nearly ten o'clock. Aren't you guys catching the midday train?" Andy asked.

"Midday train to where? My birthday dinner is cancelled, remember?" I said.

"Listen, May. I think you and Dad need to have a chat," Andy said.

I rolled over to face him. "You were there last night. Dad said the conversation was over!"

Andy shook his head. "Mum and Dad were talking for hours in the kitchen last night. I think Mum persuaded him to have a conversation about your degree."

"You know it's not actually about the degree, right?" I said. "University feels like a lifetime away. It's about–"

There was a knock on the door. "May, can I speak with you?" It was Dad.

"Come in," I said.

Andy took it at his cue to leave and took Jenny (who wasn't happy about leaving her bed) with him.

Dad hovered at the door. If he thought I was going to break the silence, he had another thing coming.

"I . . . your mother wanted us to have a chat about last night," he began.

"*Mum* wanted us to chat?"

"I did not explain myself very well last night. It's important that you know I'm not seeking to control your life. In fact, the opposite is true. I want you to have control over your life. And the way to do that is by studying a solid subject."

I crossed your arms. "So, you're not actually sorry? I thought you were here to apologise!"

"I have not finished, May. Your mother and I . . . we never want you to struggle. Not like we have. Everything we do is for you," he said, his voice cracking with emotion.

"I know how hard you work. And I'm grateful, I really am. But I should still get a say in my own future, Dad," I said.

"But you do get a say! You can study a variety of subjects: Medicine, Law . . ."

"Ahem!" A loud fake coughing sound came from behind my door. It could only be one person.

I smirked. "Mum, did you have something to add?"

Mum peeked around the door. "I was just passing in the corridor. What your father means to say is that you can study whatever you like at university."

Dad sighed. But he didn't disagree. This was progress.

I smiled. "Thanks. And I'm sorry for blowing up over dinner last night. I guess the pressure got too much . . ."

Mum reached over to the bunk bed and ruffled my hair. "I just wish you said something sooner."

Dad cleared his throat. "Happy birthday, May," he said. "Now get dressed otherwise you'll miss the train."

*

I'd arranged to meet Sunita at the train station. It would take an hour to get to Croydon, then a short bus ride to Auntie Vivian's restaurant. We drove to the train station (me, Jen, Mum, and Dad – Andy had a shift he couldn't miss) but when we got there, Dad stopped the car and didn't say anything. It was kind of weird.

"Our train leaves in ten minutes . . ." I said.

"You're not going to Auntie Vivian's," Mum said quietly.

She handed me an envelope which I opened in the backseat. It was a folded piece of paper. I read the top line.

The first thing I saw was the words Bright Stars Academy. They were tickets to Dawn's show!

"Wait. I'm going to see Dawn in London?!" I said. "But what about dinner? And Sunita?"

Mum beamed at me from the front seat. "I think we can skip the family dinner this year."

"Sunita was in on the surprise, too!" Jenny said. "You're going to the show together."

I resisted the urge to cry. Why was my life suddenly so amazing in the last twenty-four hours?!

"Thank you sooo much!" I squealed.

"You have your sister to thank. It was her idea," Dad said.

I gave Jenny a big hug and she pushed me away. "Don't be weird," she said. But she was smiling from ear-to-ear.

When I saw Sunita at the station, it was all I could do to not run down the platform. "I can't believe you tricked me!"

"I did no such thing! I just did what Jenny told me to do. She's very persuasive, you know," Sunita said.

The plan was that Mum and Jen would drop us off at the theatre while they spent the evening in Chinatown. It gave Mum the chance to pick up some much-needed supplies for the takeaway (so she says), so everyone was happy.

Sunita tucked her arm into my mine. "I have so much to tell you about."

"What, chatting until midnight last night wasn't enough?" Mum said.

"It's not the same over the phone, Mrs Chu!" Sunita said. She turned to me. "It all started when I tried to buy chicken at the butchers . . ."

CHAPTER NINETEEN

GIFTY

I had a plan, and it all started with knocking on the living room door. If Grandpa wasn't in bed or in the kitchen for mealtimes, he was in the living room watching TV. Although I don't think he actually watched it. It was just on in the background.

I bit the bullet and knocked on the door. Silence, at least for a few seconds.

"Come in," Grandpa said.

I walked in and prepared to say my rehearsed piece. "Morning Grandpa, I need your help in the shed. Do you have a minute?"

He muted the television show. "Oh . . . take what you like from the shed. I don't go there any more, Gifty," he said quietly.

"It'll only take a minute. Please?"

Reluctantly he eased himself off the armchair and stood up straight. "Well, I can spare a few minutes."

We walked to the bottom of the garden, and I opened the shed door. I walked in but he stood outside. It was like there was some forcefield stopping him from entering.

"What do you need, Gifty? I can tell you from here."

I sighed. This was going to be trickier than I thought. "Come in, Grandpa. I want to show you something."

I took him by the hand and led him into the shed.

"Why didn't you finish that painting? It's really good," I said.

He touched the canvas of the fruit bowl painting, tracing fingers through the dust. "I'd forgotten about this one," he said.

Then he noticed the set-up. I'd been in the shed earlier and cleared a space on the table. I'd filled a jam jar with fresh water and laid out the paintbrushes. The only thing missing was him.

"Oh, I can't, Gifty. My hip . . ."

"But there's a chair! If you can sit in the armchair all day, you can sit here," I said. "I don't think it's the hip that's stopping you from painting."

To my surprise, he smiled. "You know, you have Gillian's tenacity."

"Why did you abandon your shed? This place is awesome!"

"I'm glad you like it, pet," he said. "I used to spend every bit of my spare time in here. It drove your granny up the wall. But then I slipped on the garden flagstone, fell, and shattered my hip. I could barely walk for weeks."

"That sounds really hard," I said. "I sprained my ankle once and I had to stay in bed for several days. It was so boring."

Grandpa chuckled. "Yes. It was very boring. But the worst part wasn't the pain or the boredom. It was that I lost it."

"Lost what?"

"My drive. That feeling that made me excited to get out of bed and create something new," Grandpa said. "I tried to get it back. This painting was a final attempt. But the feeling wasn't there."

I thought for a second. "So you haven't lost your ability, you've lost your passion?"

Grandpa nodded. "I couldn't have put it better

myself. It's gone and I don't know if it'll ever come back."

I cast my mind back to the start of the summer. After the fancy dress nightmare, the last thing I wanted to do was sit at a sewing machine or create something new. Even though that was the thing I loved doing more than anything. It wasn't until I came here that my creativity made a return.

Maybe that would be the solution to Grandpa's problem too?

"Grandpa, I have an idea. We're going to take a little trip after lunch," I said.

I told Granny my idea and she insisted on driving us the few minutes to the village square because of Grandpa's hip. I think he could've managed the short walk just fine, but she wanted to be part of the adventure.

We pulled up at the village square and I saw it. The mural. I'd been avoiding this place for the past week, so I hadn't seen the progress Ellie had made.

I got out of the car and yelled. "Hey, Ellie! Need a hand?"

She ignored me and carried on painting. The once-white wall was slowly transforming into an incredible mural: a beautiful lake scene, serene and calm.

I walked up to Ellie and tapped her on the shoulder.

"Jesus! You made me jump," she said, removing her AirPods. "Oh, it's you," she smiled.

"I was wondering if you still needed a hand painting? I have some volunteers."

Ellie nodded. "Always. Pick up a brush."

"Did you know that my grandpa is a painter? He has an incredible studio," I said.

"No way!" Ellie said, brightening. "Well in that case, I trust you with the biggest brush."

She handed him a large brush and he took it. It wasn't like he could turn it down.

To her credit, Ellie didn't seem to mind me and my grandparents muscling in on her mural. She assigned us each a different section of the wall. I got on the ladder and painted the clouds in the sky while Granny and Grandpa filled in the trees.

We worked quietly, each of us absorbed by our own section of the mural. Minutes rolled into an hour before I realised my legs were a little sore from standing for so long.

"I can't believe you've out-painted me on my own

mural," Ellie said. "Those clouds look so realistic."

"Thanks, Ellie. I've never painted a mural before," I said.

"You're a natural," she smiled.

I sat on the bench next to Grandpa and took a good look at the mural.

"It's coming together brilliantly!" he said. There was a light in his eyes that wasn't there before. "Even your granny is enjoying herself. She never used to bother with painting."

"That's great, Grandpa."

"You're very talented, Gifty. I'm surprised. The art gene bypassed Gillian completely," he chuckled.

I laughed. Mum had many talents, but artistry wasn't one of them.

"I'm glad you've made a new friend. Let me know if you want us oldies to go home," he said with a wink.

I blushed. "That's okay. I'm just glad to see you painting."

We painted for a couple more hours then Granny said she had to get home to make dinner. She invited Ellie to join us, and she eagerly agreed. She just had to go home and drop off her painting equipment.

She met us at the house a few hours later. Even though I was nervous about having a cute girl over (did it count as a date if your grandparents were there?), I didn't feel the need to radically overhaul my wardrobe or do something new with my hair. I hadn't known Ellie for long, but I felt so comfortable with her.

I did swap my paint-stained sweater and old jeans for my mustard dungarees. Suddenly, they didn't seem so babyish any more. They felt just right for me.

Ellie arrived just as I was helping Granny make the salad dressing (apparently my 'nimble fingers' were perfect for peeling garlic cloves). I answered the door with garlicky fingers, but Ellie didn't seem to mind. She gave me a hug and presented Granny with a bunch of fresh-picked heather.

Grandad was so animated during dinner. He wanted to hear all about Ellie's mural and where she got the inspiration from. He said the painting was just what the village square needed.

We sat down to a massive shepherd's pie. I had no idea how Granny knocked it together so quickly.

"At the rate we're going, I'll be finished several days early. How long are you here for, Gifty?" Ellie asked. I think she was trying to sound casual.

My heart pounded. "My train's booked for Monday. So four more days," I said.

Ellie nodded and looked down at her plate. "That's not long," she said quietly.

"Your mum and dad must be missing you like mad," Granny said.

"I miss them too," I said. "And my best friends. All four of us have been apart for the entire summer. One of them, Dawn, is having her London stage debut on Saturday! I'm so proud of her."

"Wow! Makes sense that your friends are just as talented as you," Ellie said.

"Don't you want to see your friend's show?" Grandpa asked. "We could rearrange your train ticket."

My tummy twinged. "More than anything. They'll all be there, I imagine. But Mum and Dad would never let me roam London on my own. They're way too overprotective." I pushed my food around my plate. "Anyway, I'm having a really good time here! I'll be sad to leave."

"Oh, let's not talk about leaving already," Granny said. "It feels like you've only just arrived," she sniffed.

"Don't get upset, Granny! I've still got four more

days," I said.

"Then we'd better make them count," Ellie smiled.

After dinner, I walked Ellie back to the village square. It was still light out at eight o'clock, so we took our time walking and talking.

"So I noticed you don't spend much time with those girls anymore," Ellie said.

"Honestly? They were kind of boring. And mean. But I didn't know anyone else here, and I was lonely," I said. It was the truth.

Ellie laughed. "I'm glad you realised that. Maybe we should swap numbers . . . so if you get lonely, you won't be tempted to hang out with them."

I screwed up my face. "Believe me, I won't be hanging out with them again!"

Then I realised what Ellie was doing. *She wants your number, doofus.*

"Oh! Yeah, good idea," I said.

I handed her my phone and tried not to smile too hard. Our fingertips brushed and a thousand butter-flies let loose in my stomach. She had to like me as more than just a friend, right?

She handed back my phone and I saw that she'd saved her number as 'Ellie' followed by a tonne of emojis: painter's palette, heart eyes and sparkles.

"Just in case I don't see you before you leave," Ellie began, "can I kiss you goodbye?"

Okay. She definitely liked me as more than just a friend.

I nodded. "I'd . . . yes!"

Then she leaned in and kissed me softly, gently on the lips. It was like kissing a cloud.

I thought my first kiss would be nerve-wracking, but this was anything but. It was as natural as painting a starry night on canvas or singing in the shower, but way more fun.

She pulled away gently. "It's getting dark. Your granny will never have me over for dinner again if you come home late," Ellie chuckled.

We said goodbye and, even though I have no memory of the journey, I walked home in a bubble of happiness.

*

It was Saturday morning, the crack of dawn, and I was being woken up by a tall grey-haired man in striped pyjamas.

"Oh! Grandpa," I said sleepily. "What are you doing

here? Is Granny all right?"

"Keep your voice down! I have an idea . . . How quickly can you pack? If we leave in an hour, we can catch the early train."

"Why? It's not Monday, is it?!"

"We can make it to London by the late afternoon. For your friend's show!"

I sat up in bed. Now I was wide awake. "Are you suggesting we go to London? Together?"

"Yes. I would escort you to the theatre. That's if I wouldn't cramp your style?" Grandad asked.

I'd see my friends in just a few short hours. "This is the best idea ever!" I squealed. "But what about Mum and Dad?"

Grandad waved his hand dismissively. "Bah. Gillian worries too much for her own good. I'll take you to London, and you can get the train back home with your friends. Then I'll take the sleeper train back to Glasgow on Saturday night."

"You've thought of everything," I smiled.

Grandpa shrugged. "Couldn't sleep. So, what do you say?"

I flipped off the duvet. "I need to pack, fast."

CHAPTER TWENTY

DAWN

Today was the day. The morning of the Extras. Despite my nerves, it felt so good waking up to see my group chat with the girls alive and kicking again.

May and Sunita said they were all sorry to be missing the show. I wished May happy birthday and told her to eat an extra dumpling for me. I was sad that they couldn't make it, but my overarching feeling was the guilt twisting my stomach.

Mum was driving to Auntie Pat's house that morning. And she was expecting to see me on stage, singing one of Dad's songs.

"It's not going to happen, Dawn," I muttered to myself.

Some delusional part of my mind truly believed

that I would make everything right. That I would find some perfect solution that allowed me to keep everyone happy. But that wasn't possible.

I should be excited. This was the first time I was singing on stage in a real theatre! Not just some school play or assembly.

The doorbell rang. It was only nine o'clock. I prayed it was a postman because I wasn't ready to face–

A knock on the door. "Morning! Anyone awake?"

It was definitely Mum. I got out of the sofa bed and answered the door. She looked so happy to see me.

"How's my superstar? I've missed you sooo much!" She squealed and gave me a massive hug.

I couldn't hug back. I was tormented my guilt. Tears filled my eyes.

"Oh, sweetheart? What's the matter? I'm here now," Mum said.

"Do you . . . want a cup of tea?" I asked before running to the kitchen.

I had to get out of there. I couldn't even look Mum in the eye.

I filled the kettle up with water and put it on to boil. When it had boiled, I emptied it out and filled it up again. I wanted to freeze time.

I heard Mum, Auntie Pat and Kiana chatting in the living room. They hadn't seen each other in years and had lots of catching up to do. Good, that bought me more time. I paced the kitchen floor trying to think of a plan.

"Darlin', are you making tea or what?" Auntie Pat called from the living room.

"Coming!" I said.

I couldn't hold off any longer. I brought the tea tray in a few minutes later. My hands were shaking so hard that one of the mugs spilled over.

"Is everything alright, sweetheart?" Mum asked.

"I lied! I lied about everything," I blurted out.

Kiana rolled her eyes. Auntie Pat and Mum looked equally as confused. Well, Mum looked more worried than confused.

"Dawn, can you explain what's going on?"

"I'm . . . not singing one of Dad's songs tonight. At the Extras," I said.

Auntie Pat took the tray. "I'll take this next door. Kiana? A hand please."

"But Mum! It's about to get juicy," Kiana protested.

"Now!" Auntie Pat said firmly.

I plonked myself down on the sofa while Kiana

sidled out of the room. "Good luck," she muttered under her breath.

"Can you tell me what's going on?" Mum asked. "Did the school have a problem with you singing reggae? They can be such snobs–"

"It wasn't the school, Mum. I . . . didn't want to. I joined the Musicals class instead, so I'll be singing with them."

Mum was quiet for a second. "But I thought you loved our music? We always thought you were born to sing your father's songs."

"Don't take this the wrong way, Mum. But I think that's the problem? You and Dad decided this for me. I never had any say in the matter," I said.

Mum leaned back in the sofa, processing this brand-new information. "Forgive me but I'm confused. You don't like singing at all?"

"No! I do like singing. In fact, I love it. Acting, too," I said. "But just not the same sort of singing you love. I'm really sorry, Mum."

"Why are you sorry, sweetness?" Mum asked.

"Because . . . because . . . you gave up everything for me," I said. "So it's only fair that I do what I can to make you happy. Isn't it?"

Now Mum looked really confused. "Where on earth did you get that idea from? All I ask of you is that you take your schoolwork seriously and keep your room tidy. It's not your job to make me happy."

"So you don't want me fulfil Dad's dream?" I asked. "Because I kinda got the feeling you did."

Mum sighed. "I can see why you felt that way. And maybe I imposed a little too much on you. But I only wanted you to do it if it made *you* happy."

"Really?"

"Of course!" Mum leaned over and gave me a massive hug. "Losing your dad was the hardest thing I've ever experienced. But getting to raise you is the most joyous. Your happiness is everything to me."

It was on the tip of my tongue. I had to say it.

"I'm glad you said that, Mum. Because I think I want to go to drama school all year round," I said. "In London."

Mum chuckled. "This summer has made you bold as brass. Now, that we will have to talk about another time."

*

I was standing in the backstage area with Dante and

Haniyah. I had posted in the group chat that I was about to go on stage, and could the girls wish me luck, but no one replied. I guess they were too busy at May's birthday party.

Good. I'm glad she was having a nice birthday. And I had several people to support me: Mum assured me she'd be as close to the front as possible with Kiana and Auntie Pat.

"Have we got time for a mini prayer circle?" Dante asked.

The round of applause for the last act filtered through to the backstage.

"I guess not," Haniyah laughed.

"Whyyyyy am I so nervous? It's just one song!" I said. "It was never like this in school."

"Aw, it's baby's first stage fright," Dante smiled. "You'd better get used to it. There's plenty more performances in your future."

I took a deep breath. "Guys, I just want to say how much I've loved doing this with you. It was so hard leaving my friends for the summer, but–"

Haniyah rolled her eyes. "Don't tell me she's getting all sentimental on us?"

"Doesn't she know we're from East London?"

Dante said.

I smiled. "Fine. You get my point."

Dante squeezed my hand and mouthed 'love you' silently.

"Break a leg, chaps!" Fletcher said. "And don't embarrass me."

We walked in single file to the stage, just as we'd rehearsed for weeks. I took my spot on the stage, my eyes adjusting to the dark. Kiana waved and caught my eye; she was standing next to Mum and Auntie Pat.

Then someone else waved. Three people.

My heart jumped, but it wasn't down to nerves. Because there, standing next to Mum, were my three best friends in the world. Gifty, Sunita and May jumped up and down with excitement and I felt like I would pop.

The music began to play. I had so many questions. I had so much to tell them!

But for now, I had one thing to do: sing.

CHAPTER TWENTY-ONE

SUNITA

It was the last weekend of the summer holiday, but that didn't dampen my mood because I was finally hanging out with my girls! They came to my house for our annual pre-school manicure fest. Gifty paints all of our nails so we have a fresh mani before we go back for the new term.

Don't get me wrong. Seeing Dawn in London was epic and all, but it's not the same as chilling in my back garden. Especially as Mum and Anand made themselves scarce for the day.

Dawn, May and Gifty arrived within minutes of each other, and I greeted them the French way, with a big kiss on each cheek.

"Err, thanks, Sunita," Dawn said, wiping away

my lip gloss.

"If I give you the biggest brownie, can I avoid the sticky kiss?" May said, holding up a Tupperware box.

"Ooh! It's a deal," I squealed. "I'm glad you didn't let that nasty neighbour stop you from baking."

May had filled us in about her summer when we went out for dinner after Dawn's show, so I knew about her brownie escapades. The four of us basically talked nonstop for six hours straight.

We laid a giant blanket on the grass and lay in the garden, trying to catch every last drop of sun before we went back to prison (well, Year 10) on Tuesday. We pooled our nail colours in the middle of the blanket and decided what we were going for.

May hovered over the chic-but-boring beige and a sparkly purple, indecision written on her face. I knew exactly what she was thinking.

"Why would you choose beige when purple glitter exists?" I teased.

"Don't tell me you're still trying to prove you're a grown-up?" Dawn added with a smile.

"Fine. Glittery purple it is!" May said. She picked up the bottle and handed it to Gifty.

"It sounds like you had such an aggy summer, May," Gifty said. "First you get into a fight with the neighbour and then you gave Scott Mallory a piece of your mind."

May laughed. "Well, when you put it like that, it sounds way more interesting. Honestly, I was kind of worried I'd have a really dull summer compared to you guys. I mean, Sunita was in a French castle."

"Yeah, and mostly bored out of my brains," I said. "I spent every day hoping for a glimpse of Thibault just so I had something to do. Let's never spend the summer apart for so long."

"Deal!" Gifty said.

"Sounds good to me," May added.

Dawn sat up and flipped up her sunglasses. "Um. I'd love to agree with you guys, but . . ."

I squinted. "But what? What could possibly be more important than spending the entire summer with your favourite girls?"

Dawn smiled. "Going to Musical Theatre school? Mum agreed to it for next summer after last week's performance!"

"Okay, that definitely is more important!" I said.

"Congrats, Dawn! But I'm not surprised," May

said. "You killed that show last weekend. I couldn't have asked for a better way to spend my birthday."

"It was so nice of Jenny and Andy to organise that for you," Dawn said.

"Right?" I said. "I'm lucky if I get a card from Anand, let alone an epic birthday surprise."

"May's nails are done. Who wants to go next?" Gifty asked.

Both me and Dawn got up and scrabbled for the spot nearest Gifty. She beat me by a hair and sat down in May's spot.

"Gifty, how do you feel about nail art?" Dawn asked.

"What did you have in mind?"

"I want a lion on each thumb. Just like in *The Lion King*!" Dawn said excitedly. "So every time someone looks at my thumb and asks me about it I have an excuse to tell them all about my summer."

Gifty raised one eyebrow. "Um, it sounds intricate. But I'll do my best."

"You know, Dawn, I had no idea you were so into musical theatre," May said, blowing on her sparkly nails. "Why did you keep it quiet?"

Dawn shrugged. "I guess I thought it was kind of babyish? I was embarrassed to admit that that *The*

Lion King was my favourite soundtrack. But I'm so glad I spoke up about being a musical theatre nerd – it changed my entire summer. And Mum was totally cool with me focusing on that instead of the guitar. In fact, she said it's what Dad would have wanted for me: to be happy."

"Aww," we all said in unison. I loved hearing Dawn talk about her dad in such a nice way, especially as she didn't mention him much.

"I don't think being into Disney movies is embarrassing, but I get what you mean," May said. "I was embarrassed about working in the takeaway for ages, and Scott going out of his way to be mean at the party didn't help."

"I've never understood that," I interrupted. "You get paid to be surrounded by delicious food!"

"And Lucas . . ." Dawn said, wriggling her eyebrows suggestively.

May blushed. "That's a nice bonus too. Anyway, after Scott tried to bribe me to do his homework, I actually felt embarrassed for *him*."

"Still think you should have pocketed the cash, though," I said quietly.

"Sunita!" May gasped.

"Kidding!" I said. "But he lowkey deserved to be scammed."

"Done!" Gifty said. "Two thumb lions complete."

It was finally my turn to have my nails painted. I dithered between Vamp Red and Gleaming Gold. Vamp Red was more *Femme Fatale*, but I'd left that behind in France. I figured that Gleaming Gold would be more eye-catching, so I went for that.

"I wish I'd shouted at those nasty girls who grabbed my hair," Gifty said quietly. "Instead, I slipped out quietly without saying anything."

"That's not true," I said. "You told them to stop, didn't you?"

"Yeah! And it was three against one," Dawn said. "I once had a random person tug at my braids on the bus and I didn't say a single thing. I was just too shocked. You've got no reason to feel bad."

Gifty smiled. "Thanks, guys. It was the only downside of a pretty awesome summer. And it was all worth it for meeting Ellie."

"Oooooh!" Sunita said. "When are you going to introduce us? We need to vet her to make sure she's good enough for you."

Gifty turned bright pink. "We're not anywhere near

that stage yet! But I want to persuade Mum and Dad to visit Scotland for Christmas. Grandpa's making a work space in his art shed just for me!"

"At least you'll have something to do when the Wi-Fi is bad," May said. "I hated that we all couldn't chat together like we used to."

"It was the worst," I groaned. "All of those jokes and funny stories went to waste! My family didn't appreciate them at all."

"I definitely missed your sense of humour, Sunita," May said. "I thought you went a step too far with the *Teletubbies* fancy dress idea, but I would've given anything to hear one of your jokes over the summer."

"Too far? When you will guys realise there's no such thing," I said.

Gifty laughed. "Not everyone has your confidence, Sunita! I genuinely thought I'd have to switch schools after Holly's party."

"Believe it or not, I did try to tone it down while I was in France," I said. "I didn't want my new step-family to think I was totally eccentric. But it was just so *boring*."

"If there's one thing I've learnt this summer," Dawn said, "it's that trying not to be yourself is such hard work."

"That is so true," Gifty said. "It made Grandpa so happy when I persuaded him to do his artwork again. I'm glad I didn't let the costume party stop me."

"Why would it have stopped you?" Dawn asked. "Your costumes were incredible. Like, you could have sold them in a shop."

Gifty sighed. "Because of the way everyone looked at us when we walked into the room! I felt so embarrassed afterwards. I couldn't even look at my sketchbook for weeks in Scotland. There was some weird mental block on my creativity."

I couldn't help but feel guilty. "I'm sorry, guys. I never thought my silly fancy dress idea would be so controversial."

Gifty shrugged. "There's nothing to be sorry about. In a weird way, I'm glad it happened. Being openly laughed at was one of my biggest fears, and I lived to tell the tale. Who knows what else I can survive? Maybe I'm stronger than I thought."

"That's such a beautiful way to put it, Gifty," May said. "I might steal that for my future novel."

"It's all yours!" Gifty said. "Your nails are done

now, Sunita."

I held up my gleaming gold fingers and they twinkled in the sunlight. "Gorge! I love them."

"Now it's my turn," Gifty said, rummaging through the nail colours. We watched silently as she picked out four colours: Red, Purple, Yellow and Green.

"Ooh, are you doing a rainbow?" Dawn asked. "That's such a good idea."

"Not quite! It's been a while since Holly's party and people might have forgotten about our epic costumes. I figured I'd better remind them," Gifty said.

"That's my girl!" I said.

When our nails were dry, we scarfed down May's brownies and took turns trying to guess what teachers we'd have in Year Ten.

"I don't care who I have, as long as we're in a few classes together, all four of us," I said.

"Well, no one else but me took Art," Gifty said.

"And no one else but me took Drama," Dawn retorted.

"Did anyone take History?" May asked nervously.

"Of course not!" We replied at the same time.

May sighed. "At least we have PE together."

"Phew!" Gifty said. "I never thought I'd be grateful for PE."

"Guys, you're missing the point of this whole summer," I said. "It doesn't matter if we don't have one hundred percent of our classes together. Just as long as we have postcards . . ."

ACKNOWLEDGEMENTS

I am so unbelievably grateful that I get to call myself an author; nothing makes me happier than writing optimistic and joyful books for teens. Many people helped me along the way and it is such an honour to thank them here.

Biggest of thanks to my agent Lauren for your support and smarts. I'm so grateful you're on my team! Thanks also to everyone at Bell Lomax Moreton.

Huge thanks to everyone at my publisher Knights Of, especially my wonderful editor Eishar. Working with you is an absolute dream. Thank you for understanding what type of writer I am and bringing out the best in me. Thank you to Sophie and Robyn Smith for the beautiful cover – I love it!

I want to sincerely thank the schools and librarians who championed my earlier books – your support boosted my confidence to no end. Thank you for inviting me to your schools and for the privilege of allowing me to meet your students. You are the unsung heroes of the children's book world.

A massive thank you to my Equal Writes crew for providing much-needed feedback on my messy first draft. Charlotte, Elizabeth, Naina, Sara, Grace, Flo, Sara and Emma: you are the best writer's group a girl could ask for.

Thank you to my friends for their ongoing love and support. I feel so lucky to have you all in my life. Extra special thanks to Melissa, Mel, Sam, Sareeta, Leanne and Danielle for the love, support and group chat laughs.

Thank you to my family around the country and the world – your belief in me fuels me every day. Thank you to my in-laws/housemates Robin and Howard for letting me use your attic as my office. You guys are the best.

I'm especially grateful to my aunties (Abigail, Sonia, Monica and Jackie), my cousins, my nephew Maxwell, and my sisters Zaire, Antonia, Shakana and Zion for their love and support. I hope I have made you proud.

Hugest of thanks to my wonderful Mum. Thank you for my first library card, for sparking my love of reading and for everything you did to make my teen years so much easier. Thank you for believing in me long before I believed in myself.

Finally, I'd like to thank my husband Michael for being the best friend I could ask for. Thank you for your unwavering support in every area of my life.

ALEXANDRA SHEPPARD

AUTHOR

Alexandra Sheppard is a children's author from North London. Her debut novel *Oh My Gods* was published by Scholastic and featured in Buzzfeed, Refinery29 and The Guardian's Summer Reading List. Alex then wrote *Fly High Crew* in collaboration with the Banjo Brothers, which was published by Scholastic in April 2021. *Happy Here*, an anthology of 10 stories from Black British authors and illustrators, featuring Alex was published in August 2021 by Knights Of.

ROBYN SMITH
ILLUSTRATOR

Robyn Smith is a Jamaican cartoonist best known for her mini comic *The Saddest Angriest Black Girl in Town* and as the illustrator of the comic *Wash Day* by Jamila Rowser. She has an MFA from the Center for Cartoon Studies and has worked on comics for NECIR (New England Center for Investigative Reporting), the Seven Days newspaper, *College Humor* and *The Nib*. She loves cake and cats and holds onto to dreams of returning home to the ocean.

KNIGHTS OF

KNIGHTS OF is a multi award-winning inclusive publisher focused on bringing underrepresented voices to the forefront of commercial children's publishing. With a team led by women of colour, and an unwavering focus on their intended readership for each book, Knights Of works to engage with gatekeepers across the industry, including booksellers, teachers and librarians, and supports non-traditional community spaces with events, outreach, marketing and partnerships.